Take a look at what people are saying about

The Scrolls of Tilania

"An exciting read that mixes fantasy with science. A wondrous world is explored and an incredible mystery solved by young sleuths equipped with practical knowledge, amazing gadgets, and a lot of imagination. This is a smart, fast-paced and fun read for young readers and their parents."
- *Tonya Clegg, Educator*

....

"Katherine Burk and Gloria Burke are my favorite authors. I love their unique characters and unpredictable story plots. I am so glad that they wrote a second book."
- *Megan, age 11*

....

"Anyone who likes adventure will love this book. I loved the illustrations and the style of art. Also, I like that the book had a little Morse code in it."
- *Lillian, age 10*

....

"The story moves along briskly. Each new chapter drew me in and ended with a cliffhanger that made me want to read on. The book is full of ingenious imagery and hilarious detail. You'll want to read it straight through to the end."
- *Alice Feller, Writer and Psychotherapist*

....

"This summer I read *The Scrolls of Tilania*, the sequel to *Finding Mr. Ness* by Katherine Burk and Gloria Burke. I like and recommend this book to readers for many reasons. It has many details that stand out to me."
- *Ben, age 10*

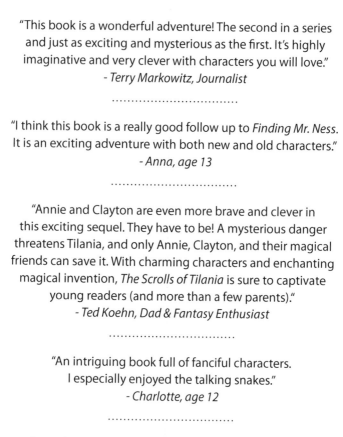

"This book is a wonderful adventure! The second in a series and just as exciting and mysterious as the first. It's highly imaginative and very clever with characters you will love."
- *Terry Markowitz, Journalist*

....

"I think this book is a really good follow up to *Finding Mr. Ness*. It is an exciting adventure with both new and old characters."
- *Anna, age 13*

....

"Annie and Clayton are even more brave and clever in this exciting sequel. They have to be! A mysterious danger threatens Tilania, and only Annie, Clayton, and their magical friends can save it. With charming characters and enchanting magical invention, *The Scrolls of Tilania* is sure to captivate young readers (and more than a few parents)."
- *Ted Koehn, Dad & Fantasy Enthusiast*

....

"An intriguing book full of fanciful characters. I especially enjoyed the talking snakes."
- *Charlotte, age 12*

....

"No other book is comparable to *Finding Mr. Ness* and *The Scrolls of Tilania* is even better!"
- *Landry, Age 10*

The Scrolls of Tilania

The Second Book In *The Tilania Travelers* Series

By Katherine Burk & Gloria Burke
Illustrations by Katherine Burk

The Tilania Travelers Series

Book 1 – Finding Mr. Ness
Book 2 – The Scrolls of Tilania

ISBN: 978-0-9907228-0-9

To order additional copies, please contact us.

Countess Press LLC
www.CountessPress.com
CountessPress@gmail.com

www.TheTilaniaTravelers.com
thetilaniatravelers@gmail.com

Especially for

Lillian & Landry

Tilania & The Underworld

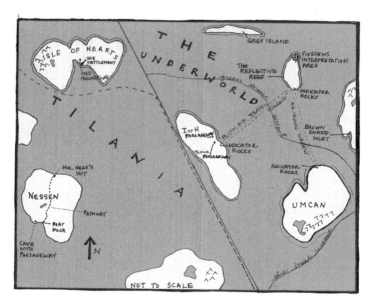

Tondore Island

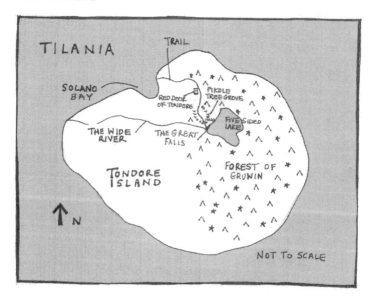

Contents

Chapter 1
The Message

Ralph bolted out from under the workshop bench, almost knocking Annie off her stool. He stood as still as a statue, the fur on his back twitching slightly.

"Clayton, look," yelled Annie, pushing her bangs out of her eyes, the way she always did when she was concentrating. "There's a weird pattern in Ralph's fur!" She scrambled to sketch it, but the image faded before she could grab a pencil.

Clayton nodded knowingly and looked at Mr. Ness. "That happened before, when Ralph and I were in your hut in Tilania," he said to Mr. Ness, who barely looked up from his notebook despite the ruckus. "But that time, Ralph's fur was shaped like the Isle of Hearts. Look," Clayton continued, tugging at Annie's sleeve. "There it is again. Draw it, quick!"

This time, Annie managed to sketch the image before it disappeared.

"That shape… I've seen it before," said Clayton, peering over Annie's shoulder.

At the mention of Tilania and the Isle of Hearts, Mr. Ness shut his notebook, dropped it on top of the pile of papers strewn on his desk, and stood up. "Need another cup," he said, lifting his coffee mug in a salute as he left the workshop.

Ever since their return to Earth, Mr. Ness refused to talk about Kalya, the Underworld, or the years he was forced to remain on Tilania. After the earthquake and Franco's death, Mr. Ness gave Kalya all the possessions he had on Tilania: his old notebook, his hut on Nessen, his research boat, The Jenny N, even his weathered binoculars from his college days.

"Clayton, get the stamp! Let's see if Kalya knows about this," Annie said, holding up the drawing.

Kalya was a Fivskew, a sea animal who looked like a cross between a turtle and a crab. Fivskews, like most  creatures of the Underworld, did not like to leave home. They preferred to stay put and learn about other worlds from the enigmatic messages displayed on the surface of the Reflective Reef. It took many years of study to acquire the skills necessary to interpret them correctly.

However, Kalya was different. He was adventurous. His trip to Earth with Annie to prevent Dennis from stealing the stamp had been the most exciting time of his life.

"*Arf! Arf!*" Ralph barked excitedly, staring at the microscope.

"We're getting the stamp," Annie reassured him, scratching the scruff of his neck. Even though Ralph couldn't talk on Earth like he could on Tilania, Annie and Clayton still managed to understand what he meant.

"*Arf!*"

"Where is it…" Clayton mumbled, rummaging through the left top drawer of the workshop bench for the rowboat stamp.

"Didn't you put it back in the dish?" Annie asked sharply.

"Er…wait, here it is," Clayton said, trying to smooth out the stamp's wrinkled corner without Annie noticing.

The stamp with the red rowboat on it was magical. Annie and Clayton had found it last fall when they were searching for something to examine with the microscope they had assembled. When they peered through the eyepiece and looked at the stamp, they were amazed to see an old man sitting inside the rowboat. It was Mr. Ness who had disappeared ten years before! He was waving his hands and shouting for them to come aboard.

And that's exactly what they did! They jumped inside the stamp and into Tilania!

Now that they were back on Earth, Annie and Clayton used the stamp to receive messages from Kalya, who had remained in Tilania. Kalya would write on the side of the rowboat with white chalk. His messages were short and predictable. He always wrote about the same thing, the progress he and his team of scientists were making to upgrade Keriam, the weather machine of Tilania's Underworld.

The last message, sent three days before, had only one word, "Finished!" Annie and Clayton knew what that meant. Kalya and his team of scientists had completed Keriam in time. Now the force of The Tidal Wave could be weakened and the Underworld saved.

Clayton clipped the stamp to the microscope stage and looked through the eyepiece.

Trouble! Scrolls. Keepers can't!
Suspicion, Disruptors! Assist
POST-HASTE!!

"What? Gimme that," he said, trying to grab Annie's drawing.

"First, tell me why you need it," she demanded, reacting more like a bossy older sister than part of a mystery-solving team.

"Kalya's message is really weird," Clayton answered, carefully copying out the undecipherable words. "Look at this," he said, showing Annie the paper.

"Is it in Fivskewese?" asked Annie.

"I don't know," said Clayton. "Mr. Ness, what do you think?"

Mr. Ness, who had just returned to his desk with his steaming cup of coffee, brushed the paper away.

"Don't you want to see?" Clayton persisted.

Mr. Ness relented and took the paper. His eyes narrowed and fixed on Clayton as he asked, "Where did you get this?"

"It was written on the rowboat," Clayton exclaimed. "It's from Kalya."

Mr. Ness flipped over the paper and held it up to the window.

"I get it!" Annie blurted out. "Mirror writing!"

"That's Brown Snake Inlet at the top," Clayton noticed, still trying to decode the message.

Annie read the message aloud:

"Trouble! Scrolls. Keepers can't! Suspicion, Disruptors! Assist POST-HASTE!!"

"What does it mean?"

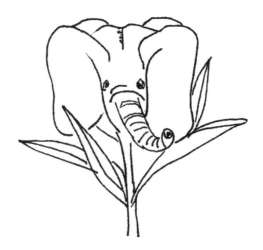

Chapter 2
The Disruptors

"'Assist post-haste?' That sounds like the brown snake," Clayton said.

"What brown snake?" Annie asked.

"Remember? The snake who helped me map Grey Island."

"Sure, I remember. You rode on his back. Grey Island is the only place where no water Travel Currents flow," Annie replied.

The Travel Currents were constructed for rapid transport between the main destinations in the Underworld. There were air currents and water currents. The air currents worked like a pulley system. As soon as an air current reached its destination, it slowed, turned, and began its return trip. The water currents traveled in one direction only.

"You told me the brown snake was one of the few survivors of The Tidal Wave, but I didn't know he talked like that," Annie continued.

"Yeah, he uses old fashioned words when he speaks. The brown snakes learned to speak English from the old books in the Isle of Hearts settlement."

"I'm pretty sure post-haste means super fast," Annie said, pushing back her bangs. "Where's the dictionary?"

Clayton began searching through the stacks of textbooks scattered on the shelf above Mr. Ness's workbench. "Found it," he said, retrieving a thick, faded red book from one of the piles. The front cover was torn almost in two, the binding was falling apart, and the last few pages of the letter "Z" entries were missing.

Clayton found the entry for post-haste.

"It says here that the first use of post-haste was in 1538. People started writing post-haste on their letters when they wanted them delivered as fast as possible. In those days, the mail was delivered on horseback. 1538…wow, that's almost 500 hundred years ago!" Fascinated, Clayton sat down to read the rest of the entry.

While Clayton read, Mr. Ness paced back and forth, scratching the back of his head and mumbling to himself. "The Scrolls…what shenanigans are the Disruptors up to now? The Scrolls should not be disturbed, it is much too dangerous! Much too dangerous!"

Mr. Ness was a brilliant scientist with a lot of annoying habits. Talking to himself was one of them. Interrupting himself was another. His mind seemed to be a scramble of ideas he was always struggling to organize.

"Need a new dictionary. Where's that list?" he muttered to himself, shuffling through the messy stacks of paper on his desk. "Ah, here it is," he said, scribbling down something on a scrap of paper.

"Mr. Ness!" Annie said, clearing her throat. "Ahem, The Scrolls?"

"What?" Mr. Ness answered, looking startled and pausing to take a long swallow of coffee. "The snakes must be the Keepers. I'll be darned."

"Mr. Ness, what are you talking about?" Annie asked, impatiently.

Mr. Ness did not stop to answer Annie's question. Instead, he went on, "'Keepers can't'? That is unheard of! The Keepers have never failed to protect The Scrolls."

"Stop," said Annie, tugging at Mr. Ness's sleeve, the sharpness of her voice revealing her irritation. "What are you talking about?"

"The brown snakes are the Keepers. Don't you see? They can't protect The Scrolls. You both need to go to Tilania and stop the Disruptors. There's no telling what havoc they are wreaking."

"Mr. Ness, please explain what is going on!" Annie pleaded.

"The Disruptors?" asked Clayton, closing the dictionary, and for the first time, paying attention to the conversation. "Who are the Disruptors?"

Mr. Ness sat down at his workbench and swiveled his chair around to face Clayton and Annie. "The Disruptors? Well, they're hard to describe. They're kind of like sprites or imps, I suppose. You know, like when your pencil keeps breaking, or you can't find something you know you put in a certain place."

"Like when one of your socks disappears in the wash?" Annie asked.

"Exactly!" said Mr. Ness. "And it seems that someone or something is doing it," he continued, taking another long swig from his coffee cup. "Well, on Tilania and in the Underworld that someone or something is real. It's a Disruptor."

"Disruptors steal stuff?" Clayton asked.

"No, they're not thieves. They're mischievous. They're pranksters. They like to change and disrupt things just for fun. They're a nuisance."

"What do they look like?" Annie asked.

"No one knows. No one has ever seen them."

"Then how do you know they're real?" asked Clayton.

"Because whenever they do something, they always leave their mark."

"You mean, like a footprint?" Clayton asked.

"Sort of, the Disruptors leave a star-shaped mark, a sign that says they've been there."

"*Arf! Arf!*" barked Ralph.

"That's right Ralph, just like a calling card," said Mr. Ness, leaning down and patting him on the head. "Their ingenuity is downright amazing. One time they built dams on the tributaries of The Wide River on

Tondore Island. The entire valley around Five-Sided Lake was flooded. Then just like that," Mr. Ness snapped his fingers, "the dams disappeared, the waters receded, and the valley returned to normal. Except for the elephant tulips."

"What are elephant tulips?" Annie asked.

"Elephant tulips are flowers. Ralph and I named them elephant tulips because they look like tiny elephant heads stuck on the ends of flower stems. Before the flood, they never grew anywhere but on Nessen. But now they bloom every spring, all over the banks of Five-Sided Lake. I remember the first time Ralph and I spotted a clump of them in the clearing right behind the hut, I could…" Mr. Ness stopped mid-sentence and reached over to turn on the old CD player sitting in the corner of his workbench. Pete Seeger's banjo music, the only thing Mr. Ness ever listened to in his workshop, began to play.

Fortunately, Mr. Ness always kept the volume low, so Annie and Clayton were able to tune out the music if they chose. That is, except when Mr. Ness decided to sing along. Then he would turn up the volume and join in, singing and twirling round and round in his chair.

That was what he was doing now, lost in the music, having forgotten about the urgency of Kalya's message.

As he spun around, strumming an imaginary banjo, Mr. Ness didn't notice that Clayton had left the well-worn dictionary sitting on the edge of the workbench. Whomp! The old dictionary crashed to the floor. What remained of the binding cracked apart and out flew a big section of the letter "L," hitting Annie on the top of her left foot. Bending down to pick it up, she noticed some notes written in red ink in the margins. The writing reminded her of something.

"Mr. Ness…." Annie started.

"Please, just call me Herman," Mr. Ness answered, no longer spinning or singing, but still strumming his imaginary banjo. "I don't know why you kids started calling me Mr. Ness again when we got back home. Honestly, I prefer Herman."

"Okay, Mr. N…Herman. Have the Disruptors ever altered a book?" Annie asked.

"I don't know," Mr. Ness answered. "Why?"

"Maybe they're the ones who changed your notebook."

"Which notebook?" Mr. Ness asked.

"Your old notebook. The one that had all the stuff you worked on before you disappeared. I found it and brought it you in Tilania. While we were on the Isle of Hearts, it was altered. All of the new research and notes from both you and Franco were added to it; we could never figure out how. The Disruptors must have been the ones who did it!"

"It was all of the new information Kalya needed to rebuild Keriam," Mr. Ness remembered.

"Exactly. The Disruptors must have done it to help!"

"That doesn't make any sense," Clayton broke in. "Why would the Disruptors want to help Kalya?"

"They live in the Underworld. It is their world too," Annie explained. "They wanted to save it."

"You're right Annie," Mr. Ness agreed. "They wanted Kalya to succeed."

"Then why are they causing trouble with The Scrolls?" Clayton asked.

"I don't know. Something has changed," said Mr. Ness. "But one thing is certain," he went on, his voice suddenly firm and confident, "The Disruptors are meddling where they shouldn't. They must be stopped. The brown snake needs your help."

Chapter 3
Tilania

"*Arf! Arf!*" barked Ralph, tugging at Clayton's pant leg.

"You're right. It's time to go," said Clayton. "Let's jump."

The stamp with the red rowboat sat clamped on the microscope stage right where Clayton had left it after reading Kalya's message.

"*Arf!*"

"What do you mean you're not coming?" Clayton asked.

"*Arf!*"

"Why not?" Annie added.

"Ralph can't go to the Underworld," Mr. Ness answered, pausing to finish his cup of coffee before continuing. "He's staying here with me. Now, where did I put those slippers?" he asked no one in particular, bending down and reaching under the workbench. "Ah, there they are. If I can just untie these laces," he muttered, struggling to undo the knots, first on his left running shoe, then on his right.

"Wait, Herman you're not coming either?" Annie looked concerned.

"I can't go down there."

"Down where?" Clayton asked, confused. "All you have to do is jump into the stamp with us, Mr. N…I mean, Herman."

"Yes, of course. I could go to Tilania, but once I'm there, there is no way I can get to the Underworld. The Passageway isn't wide enough for me and I have the scars to prove it. And my old boat, The Jenny N, can't take me there…she can only travel in Tilania. No. The two of you go. You're the ones who can help the brown snake. Ralph and I will be here if you need us; we'll keep an eye out for your messages. Off you go!"

Annie didn't like jumping into the stamp. Just thinking about it made her feel queasy. She wanted to get it over with. So before Clayton had a chance to say, "I'll go first," she shut her eyes, counted to ten, and jumped. She flew through the air and into the stamp. Making a gentle descent, she came to rest on the middle seat of the red rowboat. Clayton followed close behind, bumping into her as he landed.

"Watch out!" shouted Annie, rubbing her shoulder. "That hurt!"

"Sorry," said Clayton. "Hey look." he went on, changing the subject and pointing to the shoreline. "There's the dock! We are on the south side of Nessen. But where's the path to Mr. Ness's hut? I can't see it."

"Me neither. It must be buried under all those vines and bushes. Remember how Mr. Ness had to keep hacking away at them with his machete to clear the path?"

"Yeah. He said that the vegetation on Nessen grows like a super weed, like in 'Jack in the Beanstalk.' Look over there," Clayton continued, pointing to a spherical ship anchored nearby. "It's The Jenny N!"

....

The Jenny N looked more like a gigantic bubble than a boat. Neither Annie nor Clayton knew why Mr. Ness had designed such a strange looking vessel, or what purpose its spherical shape served. Instead of wood or fiberglass, it was made of a thin translucent material that was transparent in places. There was a hatched door at the top, and inside, a circular staircase descended into the cabin below. When Mr. Ness lived there, one half of the cabin's interior was the living quarters, with an old couch, a reading lamp, a small table, his unmade bed with Ralph's rumpled cushion next to it, and a cooking area, which always had a sink full of dirty dishes.

The other half of the cabin was both Mr. Ness's laboratory and the boat's navigational hub. Like his workshop on Earth and his hut on Nessen, Mr. Ness's lab was always cluttered and disorganized. The large tabletop overflowed with pieces of machinery, bits of electronic equipment, and projects in different stages of completion. The shelves were stuffed with books, rolled up manuscripts, and piles of paper. A black captain's chair,

"The Jenny N" written across its back in large white letters, sat in front of an instrument panel and above it was a large illuminated screen. Annie wondered if the cabin's interior still looked as messy and disheveled now that Kalya was the captain.

"Come on, let's row over and find Kalya," said Clayton.

Annie secured the two oars into their oarlocks, while Clayton pulled the anchor aboard. Then Annie turned the rowboat around to point its bow in the direction of The Jenny N, and began to row.

"I wish there was a way to row fast without having to face backwards," she said. "Tell me if I'm going straight, okay?"

Seeing The Jenny N reminded Clayton of the first time he had been aboard and discovered Mr. Ness's little robots. When Mr. Ness returned to Earth, he left his robots behind. But, to Clayton and Annie's delight, he soon built three new ones in his workshop. They were small, metal, human-like creatures about the size of a can of soda. Even though their "brains" were in their bodies, Mr. Ness had assembled each of them with a head and an expressive face. He said that made it more fun to talk to them. Annie named them Clint, Sunny, and Bo. Clint had a dent in his forehead and Sunny always looked like she was smiling. Bo was the tallest—lanky and long limbed, like a gun-slinging cowboy. They had retractable arms and legs and could follow short voice commands. Mr. Ness programmed them to do simple chores, like making coffee. They could measure the coffee beans into Mr. Ness's coffee maker, add the correct amount of water, and turn on the switch. They also knew how to make three different kinds of paper airplanes—the Classic Dart, the Arrow, and the Stealth. The airplanes were flawlessly constructed, every fold and bend executed with perfect precision. But, even though all three robots were programmed to fly them exactly the same way, whenever Bo or Clint tried, the planes would crash to the ground. Only Sunny was able to get them to soar through the air. Mr. Ness thought the variation in resting arm length was the reason, but Annie thought Sunny just had a better attitude. "Sunny wants to fly the planes. Bo and Clint just look bored," she said one day, when the robots were turned off and recharging. Clayton agreed. While Bo and Clint slumped against each other, Sunny stood tall, alert, and ready for action.

....

"That's Kalya over there," Clayton said, pointing to a patch of churning water heading towards them. "His tentacles are beating so fast, I can't see his shell, but I'm sure it's him. I think he's shouting something."

Annie turned the rowboat around so she could see Kalya too. He was now close enough to hear.

"Drop anchor," he called out, swimming toward the rowboat. He reached out his front right tentacle, grabbed hold of the side of the boat, and climbed aboard. Settling himself on the floor next to Clayton's feet, he drew all six tentacles into his multicolored, spiral-shaped shell, and peered up at Annie and Clayton, his bright green eyes open wide in surprise.

"I didn't expect you to get here so fast. I left the message less than an hour ago!"

Clayton and Annie knew an hour in Tilania and the

Underworld didn't always equal an hour on Earth. The passage of time was unpredictable here. Sometimes it went faster than an Earth hour, and other times slower. They never knew what to expect. Clayton understood this best; when he was mapping the Underworld, sometimes five minutes felt like a day, sometimes it felt like an hour or two, and sometimes it felt like five minutes exactly.

"As soon as we saw a strange pattern in Ralph's fur, we checked the stamp and found your message," Annie explained.

"There was a pattern in Ralph's fur?" Kalya asked.

"Yeah, it was an outline of an island in the Underworld, the one with Brown Snake Inlet," said Clayton. "That's where I met the brown snake."

"The message came from him, didn't it?" Annie asked.

"Yes. It is from the brown snake," Kalya replied. "He traveled here from the Underworld this morning. He insisted I send you his message right away. I left the wording exactly the way he wrote it, but I couldn't risk the Disruptors reading it. That's why I put it in mirror writing."

Kalya leaned over the side of the boat and quickly rubbed off the chalked message with one of his tentacles. "We better be careful. No telling if the Disruptors are watching."

"Mr. Ness told us about them," said Clayton. "He said they were tampering with The Scrolls. Why is that so dangerous? Why are The Scrolls so important?"

"The preservation of The Scrolls is crucial to the balance and equilibrium of both Tilania and the

Underworld. They contain our entire history and foresee our future. Without their existence our worlds would be thrown into chaos."

"So, The Scrolls tell the future?" Annie asked.

"Not exactly. The future is written on them. But it is never told. We have always known that the brown snakes are both the recorders and the protectors of The Scrolls. The Disruptors must be endangering their safety. Nothing like this has ever happened before—it is unprecedented! You must go help the brown snake at once."

"But where is he?" asked Clayton.

"He's waiting for you at the Reflective Reef."

Chapter 4
Nocto-Vision

Annie knew exactly what to do. She turned the rowboat around and started rowing as fast as she could. "I'll head for the far side of the dock. That way we'll be near the cave and the Passageway to the Underworld."

When the rowboat was close to the shore, and the water shallow enough, Clayton jumped out, grabbed the rope tied to the bow of the boat and dragged the boat up onto the beach. "I'll get our suits," he shouted over his shoulder, racing into the cave.

Clayton reappeared a moment later, carrying two duffel bags. "Here catch," he shouted, tossing Annie hers. "Let's get ready. We can use the trees for cover."

The duffel bags contained the suits Mr. Ness had custom-made for Annie and Clayton, using fabric of his own invention. The material was extremely thin, but as strong as dragon scales—designed specifically to protect Annie and Clayton's skin from the sharp, rocky walls of the narrow, steep Passageway.

Annie and Clayton emerged from the trees dressed in their suits, their clothes stuffed into their bags. "Kalya!" Clayton shouted, looking around the cave's entrance. "Where are you?"

"Kalya!" echoed Annie.

"I'm in here, inside the cave," came a muffled reply. "I'll be out in a second. It's a bit tricky," Kalya continued, stepping out into the light. "I need to take my time." He started wiggling out of his shell, stopping when enough of his body was free to lean back onto his rear tentacles. "I have something to give you," he continued, reaching a tentacle inside his now partially empty shell. He handed Annie and Clayton each a small black object, the size and shape of a credit card.

"Our MRVDs," exclaimed Clayton.

There was no mistaking which one was Clayton's. It had a vertical crack right down the middle of its screen, and a small dent in the upper right corner. Annie's, on the other hand, looked brand new.

Mr. Ness had given the MRVDs to Clayton and Annie when they first arrived in Tilania. The MRVDs, or Multi Recording Visual Devices, were powerful computers. The data Clayton had collected on his MRVD of The Tidal Wave's destruction to the Underworld had been critical to Kalya's success in upgrading Keriam.

"It's pitch black in the cave—the perfect place to try out Nocto-Vision. I just tested it," Kayla said, holding up Mr. Ness's old MRVD. "It worked perfectly."

"Nocto-Vision?" Clayton stepped closer to get a better look.

"It's an invention Mr. Ness was working on while he was here in Tilania. It allows you to see in the dark. I found the prototype for it on The Jenny N. I made a couple of modifications to it and got it working. It is now a feature on your MRVDs."

Kalya was an accomplished inventor. Among his most renowned inventions were two devices: a TC Catapult, and a Gust Blocker. Using them made it possible to transport objects on the air Travel Currents. To do this, first the object or objects were placed on the TC Catapult. Next, the TC Catapult was wheeled into position and set exactly 32 ¼ inches from the lowest Indicator Rock. Then, in the silence between the gusts of air, a lever was pulled, throwing the object up into the Travel Current. The traveler, holding the Gust Blocker in one hand, followed in the gust of air just behind the object. When the end of the Travel Current approached, the traveler aimed and shot the Gust Blocker in front of the object he or she wanted to release. The object immediately fell to the ground.

"To activate Nocto-Vision you simply push this until you hear a click," said Kalya, pointing to an orange button on the lower right corner on his MRVD. "Why don't you give it a try?"

Annie and Clayton each held their MRVD, pushed the orange button, and waited for the click.

"That should do it," said Kalya. "You won't notice

anything out here in the sunlight. Go inside the cave and try it out. It works even if the MRVD is inside your pocket. I'll wait here by the entrance."

Annie and Clayton headed into the dark cave.

"Wow!" said Annie. "What happened? It's as bright in here as it was outside."

"Now, push the orange button again and tell me what happens," Kalya called, from outside the cave's entrance.

"I can't see a thing," said Annie.

"Neither can I," added Clayton.

"The button should be glowing orange," Kalya continued. "It is raised a little in case the back light fails. I designed it like that so you could feel it in the dark. Now go ahead and turn it back on."

"I can see perfectly again! How does it work?" asked Clayton. "It doesn't light up the room like a flashlight. It's my eyes. They're different. I can see in the dark!"

"That's right," answered Kalya. "Nocto-Vision changes the way your eyes see. It gives you night vision, like cats and other nocturnal animals have."

"Does it change our pupils or give us a tapedum lucidum?" asked Annie.

"How do you know about that, Annie?"

"I've been learning about nocturnal animals[1] for my science project," Annie answered, emerging from the cave with Clayton.

"'Tap e de' what?" Clayton asked.

"It's called a tapetum lucidum. Tapetum lucidum is

Latin. Lucidum means bright and tapetum means tapestry or cloth. Tapetum lucidum is an extra layer cats have in their eyes that lets in more light, so they can see in the dark. I don't know exactly how it works. Cats' pupils are different too. They can get a lot bigger than a human's pupils. That's another way they get more light into their eyes.[1]"

"Nocto-Vision does the same thing," said Kalya. Turn it on, and your eyes can see perfectly, no matter how dark. Turn it off, and they return to normal."

Annie and Clayton each slipped their MRVD into the small front pocket in their suit and zipped it shut.

"If I discover a pattern to the Disruptors' activities and can predict where they might strike next and what they are doing, I will contact you on your MRVDs," said Kalya. I will use Morse code so even if the Disruptors intercept the message they won't understand it. Your MRVDs have a decoding translator. But, enough talk. Time for you to go."

"Come on Annie," shouted Clayton, running back into the cave.

"Bye," said Annie reaching over and patting Kalya's shell, before rushing off to join Clayton.

"Good luck," Kalya called out after them.

....

[1] *Nocturnal animals are able to see in the dark better than humans. Their pupils are bigger and this allows more light to reach the retina at the back of their eyes. They also often have a tapetum lucidum, a mirror like membrane in front of the retina, which reflects light that has passed through the retina back through it a second time. The light sensitive cells in the retina of nocturnal animals are made up of a larger number of rods than cones as compared to humans. Rods work in low light. Many bats, nocturnal snakes, and lizards have only rods and no cones.*

MORSE CODE

Morse code is made up of dots and dashes instead of letters. MRVDs use either sound or written symbols to send Morse code messages.

The most well-known message in Morse code is SOS (· · · — — — · · ·) which means HELP!

....

International Morse Code

1. A dash is equal to three dots.
2. The space between parts of the same letter is equal to one dot.
3. The space between two letters is equal to three dots.
4. The space between two words is equal to seven dots.

Chapter 5
The Passageway

With their Nocto-Vision turned on, Annie and Clayton could see the walls of the dark, musty cave for the first time.

"Look at all these cave paintings," Annie marveled. "They're everywhere."

The paintings were of familiar Underworld scenes: the Reflective Reef, a stack of Indicator Rocks marking the beginning of an air Travel Current, and trees filled with palm fruit, to name a few.

"Tilanians must have painted these; Underworldlians don't travel," said Clayton. "The details are amazing," he added, tracing his index finger along the trunk of one the painted trees.

"I wonder how old they are," Annie said, pushing her bangs out of her eyes and squinting at the tiny, red berries on one of the painted bushes. "It's weird, I never thought about anyone else using the Passageway. Did you?"

"I know what you mean. It has an abandoned sort of feeling," said Clayton.

"We better go," said Annie.

They headed towards the steady stream of cold, damp air escaping from the Passageway entrance at the far end of the cave.

"Look at the brown snakes in this one," Clayton said, stopping at a painting next to the Passageway entrance. "I've never seen them on land before."

"That one is almost as wide around as the tree trunk it's climbing," Annie exclaimed. "You didn't tell me how huge they were!"

"Yeah, they are. They're big enough to ride. I rode snakeback all around Grey Island. Remember?"

"I guess I didn't realize they were so gigantic," said Annie. She sat down on the narrow ledge at the top of the Passageway entrance, and scooted forward to make room for Clayton behind her. Blowing her bangs out of her eyes, and taking a deep breath, she began to review the rules: "Keep your elbows in. Watch out for bumps. Careful of the second-to-last turn."

"I know. I know. I remember," said Clayton, already annoyed with Annie for being in front. He sat down behind, stretched out his legs on either side of her, and wrapped his arms around her waist. Then, together they counted to three, tucked their heads into their chests, leaned forward and pushed off, heading down the chute. The dank, cold air whistled by as they whizzed down the narrow tunnel, turning and twisting all the way, the rocky walls blurring past them. When they reached the bottom of the Passageway, they flew through the air, and came to rest with a heavy thud on the sandy beach of the Underworld.

There was no sign of The Tidal Wave's destruction anywhere. It was as if the disaster had never occurred. It was true! Kalya and his team of scientists had rebuilt Keriam in time. The ocean sparkled in the sunlight and the air was alive with the warble and trill of bird song. Everywhere flowers were in bloom.

Annie and Clayton ran to the three neatly stacked Indicator Rocks, which marked the beginning of the yellow air Travel Current.

Clayton, determined to be first this time, stood next to the Indicator Rocks, waited for a silent pause between the gusts of air, and stepped into the path of the air Travel Current. It swept him high into the sky and propelled him forward out to sea. He flew through the air, his arms reaching out in front, his legs stretched out behind. When he looked back over his shoulder to wave to Annie, she wasn't there!

Annie had waited for the pause after the next gust of air, and stepped into the path of the air Travel Current. But nothing had happened. Confused, she stepped out to try again, but the gusts of air had stopped. She saw Clayton flying farther and farther over the water into the distance. The Travel Current was obviously still working for him.

She searched the beach all around the Indicator Rocks to see if something was blocking the gusts of air. There was no indication anywhere that anything was wrong. She had no idea what to do to get the Travel Current working again. Frustrated, she sat down to write Clayton an MRVD message in Morse code.

That is when she noticed a tiny antenna about two inches long protruding from the sand at the base of the largest Indicator Rock. Brushing away the sand, she uncovered a rectangular speaker with the word "SERVICE" written in large red letters across its front, and a red arrow pointing to a switch.

She flipped it on.

Chapter 6

Thila Mae

There was a brief silence, then the faraway sound of wind chimes. The clinking grew louder and louder, and harsher and harsher. Annie flipped the switch off, but the racket continued. She covered her ears and tried to block it out. The wailing of a siren started. A shadow passed overhead.

Annie looked up and saw an enormous pink bird, so large that its outstretched wings blocked out the sun. It darted from tree to tree, hardly landing before it flew off again, its wings flapping wildly. Finally, it came to rest right beside Annie, balancing on one long skinny leg, while the other bent back and kicked the speaker hard, knocking it over and shutting it off.

The bird was wearing a green and yellow plaid cap, a brown and white polka-dot vest, and brown laced-up work boots with long purple socks. A leather tool belt, with a metal box hanging off one end, was buckled up just under its wings. It stood so tall, it had to bend down and stretch out its neck so it could talk to Annie face to face. And when it did, Annie noticed a strange pendant dangling from its neck. It was shaped in a half circle, like a horseshoe worn for good luck, except this one had a little tail sticking out at the bottom, like on the letter Q.

"Thilamaeteknision," it chattered. "Adyursirvise. Whasdemadder?'"

"Excuse me," Annie answered. "I can't understand you."

"Thilamaeteknision," it repeated. "Adyursirvise. Whasdemadder?"

"Sorry," Annie replied. "Could you please speak a little slower?"

The bird swooped into the air above the Indicator Rocks and began to slowly lower a long cable with a loop at one end from the back of its tool belt, skillfully lassoing it around the base of the bottom Indicator Rock.

Then it flew back to Annie.

"Thila Mae Technician," she said. "At your service. Glad to meet you. And your name is? Not getting any gusts of air? That's the problem is it? When did it start? Did you notice anything before it happened? Any strange noises?"

There was no space between Thila Mae's questions for Annie to answer. She did manage to blurt out, "I'm Annie," before Thila Mae flew off again, landing on the top of a tall palm tree, and this time staying put. The treetop was too high for Annie to see what was happening. But she could hear Thila Mae shouting down more questions.

"Anyone with you? What did you say your name was? Been waiting long? Having problems with any other Travel Currents? Just mean the air ones. Max does the water ones.

"Almost finished. Down in a jiffy. Got to stretch out a bit first," Thila Mae continued, soaring and gliding high in the sky, making one graceful figure eight after another.

"Boy that felt good!" she said, landing at Annie's side once again. "It's been ages since I got a chance to practice. I'm so darn busy most of the time. How'd they look? It's Annie isn't it? Don't you worry, Annie, I'll get her up and running for you in no time. But I got to admit I have my suspicions. You didn't happen to notice a star-shaped mark around here did you? That's what they always leave after they've done whatever it is they're doing. Never interested in the Travel Currents before though. But you never know. Especially now. I'm starving. How about you? Wouldn't happen to have anything to eat would you? Or do you always make it a point to travel light? Can't say that I do. Need these tools. Every last one of them. And wouldn't take a step out of my workshop without my toolbox. Chicken in orange sauce, that's my all time favorite sandwich. Smothered in Brie. And lots of olives on the side. Look here! This must be my lucky day, got half a one left in my toolbox. Too busy at the last service job to finish it. Want some? Guarantee you'll like it. Made it myself this morning."

"I…my friend Clayton…he got on the Travel Current… caught a gust just before I tried," Annie said, struggling to reorder her mind in the welcomed silence that followed Thila Mae's jumbled barrage of thoughts. "They stopped before…"

"Got to wet my whistle," Thila Mae interrupted, unscrewing the top of a bright orange thermos, flinging her head back, and taking a long, noisy guzzle.

"…the gusts stopped coming," Annie continued, determined to finish what she was saying. "But Clayton didn't fall off of the Travel Current. Will he make it to the Reflective Reef?"

"Clayton, you say? The fella on the Travel Current? No problem there. Can't fall off once you're on. That's for sure. Get you caught up to him lickety-split. Don't you worry. Hold onto this hammer will ya? Big help. Whoa…it's a mess all right. Guess we got to untangle these first." Thila Mae handed Annie a large wad of tangled cables. "Give the orange one there a good yank. Hard as you can. Nope, that's not it. Better try the blue. Well, I'll be, not that one either. Give it here a sec. Let's have a look. Mmmm…yup, that's it. Just be a minute. Have a seat. Take a load off."

Annie sat down, rested her back against the nearby tree trunk, and took out her MRVD. It was her first chance to send Clayton a Morse code message. But as soon as she started to type, Thila Mae interrupted her.

"Figured it out. Gotta say, had me stumped there for a second," she said, tossing Annie the tangle of cables. Annie caught the messy tangle of cables with one hand, and stuffed her MRVD into the front pocket of her suit with the other.

Give it a try now," said Thila Mae. "Start with the red one. That's the ticket."

Chapter 7
The Reflective Reef

Clayton flew far out to sea following the path of the yellow air Travel Current. The salty spray from the waves below made him wish he was wearing goggles to protect his eyes. He was already more than halfway to the Reflective Reef, but there was still no sign of Annie. He wondered what was keeping her. Why hadn't she gotten onto the Travel Current?

Brooff! Brooff! Brooff! Low barking sounds competed with the noise of the splashing waves. Clayton looked down and saw a group of whiskered, grey sea creatures diving and frolicking in the choppy water below. Their playful antics reminded him of the sea otters he liked to watch romping and wrestling with each other near the piers in the bay at home. But these animals were larger than sea otters and seemed to be playing an organized game. Two of the players held up a net made of seaweed, while the remaining six, three on each side, used their flippers to bat a round object back and forth over the net. Was it a sea sponge? Clayton couldn't be sure. When one side failed to return the sponge, or whatever it was, the other side barked excitedly, bobbing up and down, clapping their flippers together in celebration.

Then, the "sea sponge" got caught in the net and the two players holding the net started to bark a cheer, while the other six players made loud sounds of protest. Clayton watched in amazement as the seaweed net began to grow, doubling in height within seconds. The two net holders repositioned themselves making the net taut once again. The left net holder used his flipper to dislodge the sponge, whistled, and tossed it high into the air. The game resumed.

None of the players took any notice of Clayton as he sailed by overhead on the Travel Current. He wished he could stop and watch another round of "three team otter ball", but he flew on, and the creatures and their game soon disappeared from view. Clayton's thoughts returned to Annie's mysterious absence.

He wondered if he should drop off the Travel Current, fall into the water, and swim back to the Indicator Rocks to look for her. But he quickly decided that would be a mistake. He was already more than halfway to the Reflective Reef; swimming all the way back would take too long. He also considered taking advantage of the Travel Current's circular pathway and instead of getting off at the Reflective Reef, staying on for a round trip return to the Indicator Rocks. But that was a bad choice too. Annie might have gotten on the Travel Current after all. Then they could both end up traveling around and around on it, never catching up with each other.

Lost in thought, Clayton almost missed his chance to lean away from the force of the Travel Current and drop off at the Reflective Reef before it turned to begin its return journey.

He landed on the edge of the Reef. Its rocky perimeter was dotted with tide pools that glistened in the sun. Crouching down beside the nearest pool, he peered through the clear water teeming with sea life. Starfish clung to the tide pool's creviced walls. Tiny snails crept past sea anemones that gently swayed to and fro. Brightly colored fish, some striped, others spotted, darted in and out among the coral.

A flock of squawking orange birds circled overhead. Each took its turn diving into the water, resurfacing moments later, dinner firmly clasped in its beak. A giant crab, clad in a "W" shaped orange and yellow shell, crawled up, over, and down Clayton's feet. Clayton watched as it awkwardly scuttled along on its journey. When the crab reached the steep steps that led onto the Reflective Reef, Clayton jumped up and snapped to attention, suddenly remembering why he was there.

"Hello," he called out to the brown snake. "Hello! It's Clayton. I'm here."

There was no answer. He climbed to the top of the steep, slippery stairs carved into the Reflective Reef and scanned the surrounding waters below. "Hello! Hello!" he called out again. There was still no answer. He sat down on the top step to wait. Unzipping the front pocket on his suit, he took out his MRVD, and typed a message to Annie. Then he pushed the Morse code translator key:

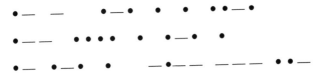

The MRVD screen flashed the words "Awaiting authentication value. Please set question and response." Then the word "Question" blinked on and off.

"Authentication value? Question and response?" Clayton puzzled to himself. "Ah!" he said aloud, as he remembered having to enter his last name in order to retrieve a message from Ralph.

Clayton typed, "classroom number," and pushed ENTER. Then he typed, "14" and pushed ENTER again. The MRVD beeped and then flashed "Delivery successful."

Chapter 8
Listen

Annie held on to the tangle of colored cables Thila Mae threw to her and yanked hard on the red one. The tangle broke apart and fell to the ground at her feet.

Thila Mae scooped up the cables, rushed to the far side of the Indicator Rocks, and began arranging the cables carefully side by side on the sand. "Blue, red, orange, white, navy. B-R-O-W-N. That'll do it. Don't know why. But never you mind. Got her going. Step right up. Let's give it a look-see."

Annie positioned herself near the Indicator Rocks, and heard the familiar whooshing gusts of air rushing by. The Travel Current was working again.

"On you get," said Thila Mae. "No time for goodbyes. Be seeing you sooner rather than later."

Annie listened for the silence after a gust of air, quickly stepped into the path of the air Travel Current, and waited for the next gust to sweep her up into the sky. But it never came. Instead there was a low, deep rumbling, followed by a loud grinding noise.

"Well I'll be. This is most unusual. Hmmm…" said Thila Mae, rummaging through her toolbox. "Most unusual."

Annie heard a faint beep, beep, beep. She reached inside the front pocket of her suit, retrieved her MRVD, and pushed the flashing green button on its surface. The screen lit up with a typed message.

"Urgent! To receive message input classroom number."

Annie hesitated, then realizing what it meant, typed "14" and pushed ENTER. The message appeared. It was in Morse code:

She pushed the Morse code translator key. The translated message read:

> AT REEF
> WHERE
> ARE YOU

She looked over at Thila Mae. Her head was buried in her toolbox and she was chattering to herself.

Annie wrote back:

TC BROKEN. DON'T WAIT FOR ME. MEET AT THE JENNY N.

She pushed the translator key, sent the coded message and starting walking towards the Passageway to begin her journey to The Jenny N.

"Whoa there! Wait a sec. Don't vamoose now. Got it all figured out," said Thila Mae. "Darned if it isn't the Bit Joiner. Take a look. Broke clear in half. And, yup, it was the Disruptors alright. No doubt about it. See this here mark in the sand?"

Annie walked over to Thila Mae and peered at the star-shaped mark. She bent down to touch it and was surprised that the mark's sandy surface felt as hard and unyielding as cement.

"Once their mark is there it's there for good," Thila Mae explained. "Bit Joiner. Who would have thought? No problem, got an extra one in here somewhere," she continued, burying her head in her toolbox again. "Found it when I was visiting the Forest of Gruwin. Been there, haven't you? Up in Tilania. Nice place. But bad bugs. Give us a hand here. Can't get this Bit Joiner tuned without you," Thila Mae went on, handing Annie a shiny metal disc with the letters N, Z, and U stamped around the edges in sparkling blue stones. "Gotta make sure the N is closest to the Indicators Rocks. Hold her steady and flat, like a compass. That's it. It'll calibrate in a sec.

"Thing about 'B-R-O-W-N,' just is what it is. Can't be anything else. Now you take, 'eleven plus two.' That's a doozie. Change those letters around and presto, you get, 'twelve plus one'. Move 'astronomers' around and, poof, you get 'moon starers'. Do you follow me?"

"Yeah. They're anagrams,"[2] Annie answered.

"Right you are," said Thila Mae, "Special ones too. They mean what they mean, if you know what I mean." Thila Mae grabbed a stick and wrote "the Morse code" in the sand and underneath it, "here come the dots." "Amazing isn't it. Even got one of my own, 'Thila Mae Technician,' that's me, 'The Tilania Mechanic.'"

"Bet that Bit Joiner is done calibrating," said Thila Mae. She rushed back to the far side of the Indicator Rocks and began tying the cables together into another messy bundle. "Keep holding that Bit Joiner, Annie. Still as a statue. Be done before you know it. Just one left to tie. That's it. Hear that whooshing noise? There you go. Got it up and running."

Annie waited for the silent pause between the gusts of air, but this time, instead of stepping in herself, she threw a small stone into the path of the Travel Current and watched it fly out over the water.

Thila Mae didn't ask Annie why she wasn't getting on herself. Instead she started flapping her wings rapidly. "Time to go. Duty calls," she said, taking off and flying high into the air. After circling twice and making three perfect figure eights, she dipped down and shouted, "Give my old friend Kalya a message. Tell him, 'Twig in virus'. Got that? 'Twig in virus.'"

Annie pushed the orange button on her MRVD to activate her Nocto-Vision, zipped it up into the front pocket of her suit, and ran to the entrance to the

---

[2] *A word or phrase formed by reordering the letters of another word or phrase, such as "the eyes" to "they see" or "listen" to "silent."*

Passageway. She climbed the narrow steps and waited to be thrown forward onto her stomach and propelled up to the top. She had experienced this rapid "upslide"[3] before, when she used the Passageway to return to Tilania. She reached the top of the Passageway at the precise moment she unscrambled the anagram. "Twig in virus" was "visit Gruwin!"

Gruwin? Annie wondered. Why would Thila Mae want Kalya to visit the Forest of Gruwin?

....

[3] *The term "upslide" was described for the first time in the camping adventure stories created and told by LGE and LME.*

Chapter 9
A Reading

Clayton searched the waters below for the brown snake. Beep, beep, beep, his MRVD sounded, indicating that Annie had returned his message. "Urgent! To receive message, input pet's name," flashed across its screen.

He typed his dog's name, "Prince," and pushed ENTER. A Morse code message appeared. He pushed the translator key. The message read:

TC BROKEN. DON'T WAIT FOR ME. MEET AT THE JENNY N.

Clayton stared at the message for a minute before realizing that TC meant the Travel Current. So that's why she didn't come, he thought. He scanned the water below one last time. There was no sign of the brown snake. Leaving his perch at the top of the stairs, he stepped carefully onto the slick, iridescent surface of the Reflective

Reef. He knelt down and pressed his palms firmly onto its surface to trigger a reading. Nothing happened. The Reflective Reef's surface remained unchanged.

The Reflective Reef was like an oracle, or fortune-teller. Among its many functions was the prediction of weather patterns and natural disasters, such as The Tidal Wave that had threatened to destroy Tilania's Underworld. The Reflective Reef was also the source of a wide range and breath of knowledge about the Underworld, Tilania, and even Earth. Kalya had explained that learning how to elicit a response and read the Reflective Reef's messages were skills that took years to acquire. Surprisingly, Clayton and Annie had successfully triggered responses from the Reflective Reef and understood the images displayed to them the very first time they traveled there.

"Hi, I'm Clayton, remember me?" Clayton began, keeping his palms on the Reflective Reef's surface. "You helped me before. The image you showed me of Annie's mom listening to the radio in her car was awesome. That's how I figured out how to trap Franco. And the picture with all those colored lines, that was a map of the water Travel Currents. Once I understood what they were, I traveled everywhere mapping the Underworld for Kalya. Now I'm here because the brown snake left me a message…"

Suddenly, a powerful jolt of energy arced through Clayton's body and the Reflective Reef's iridescent surface transformed into a brilliant blue sky. Fluffy white clouds and a gaggle of honking geese flying in a v-shaped formation glided by. Clayton watched as the blue sky darkened to black, the clouds and geese disappeared, and an image of reddish-purple light, in the shape of a horseshoe, illuminated the surface. The Reflective Reef returned to normal.

Blue sky? Clouds? Geese honking? A reddish-purple horseshoe? Clayton puzzled over the Reflective Reef's mysterious message.

"Wait, I don't get it," he called out to the Reflective Reef. "Show it to me again!"

But the Reflective Reef did not respond.

Chapter 10
Mortimer

"Master Clayton, are you in attendance perchance?" the brown snake called out from the water below.

"I'm up here," shouted Clayton, scrambling down the Reflective Reef's steps to the water's edge. "I didn't see you. The Reef...it was…"

"My good sir," interrupted the brown snake, "it is with the upmost gratitude that I bid you a heartfelt salutation," he continued, nodding his head solemnly, waving his tail from side to side. "That you have responded to our plea for help with such haste is most welcomed."

"I got here as fast as I could. What's going on? How can I help?"

"It is with regret that I bid you bring your inquiries to a halt, my dear friend," said the brown snake, interrupting Clayton once more. "Would that it were otherwise. Alas, such is the turmoil and uncertainty of these times that I must forego my response until a more propitious moment is upon us. Come, we must repair to Brown Snake Inlet without further ado. May I humbly counsel that you travel as before, on snakeback, a most expedient mode of transport," continued the brown snake, swimming towards Clayton.

"Sure," answered Clayton, wading into the water and climbing onto the snake's back.

Raising his head higher above the water, the brown snake turned slightly towards Clayton. "Please permit me to address a prior lapse in protocol," he said. "I fear I was not fully myself when last we met amidst The Tidal Wave's calamitous destruction to my beloved surrounds. Such was the depth of my sorrow. I now hasten to make amends and render a full and proper introduction. My given name is Mortimer. I am Principal Spokesnake of Brown Snake Inlet. Presently you will meet my beloved."

"Is that her, up ahead?"

"Indeed, it is she."

A smaller snake, her head and tail darkly speckled, slithered gracefully toward them. "Fond greetings to you, fine sir," she began, "I am Tallulah, wife of Mortimer. It is my great honor to at last make your acquaintance."

"Good to meet you too," Clayton replied.

"Pray tell, what of your companion, Miss Annie," Tallulah continued, in a lilting, singsong voice. "I have ventured forth so that she, too, might partake of snakeback travel, and thus hasten her journey to Brown Snake Inlet."

"She couldn't get here," replied Clayton. "The Travel Current broke. It stopped working right after I got on."

47

"Alas, I fear the Disruptors are wreaking havoc in yet more ways than first we surmised," Tallulah sang with a sigh. "Doth Miss Annie require our assistance?"

"No, not right now," Clayton replied. "She's okay. She's back in Tilania on The Jenny N with Kalya."

"Would that Miss Annie were here with us now. That such should have befallen her is most unfortunate," said Tallulah.

"These are troubled times, indeed," said Mortimer. "We know not where danger lurks. It is necessary that we exercise the utmost prudence and remain always at the ready. To this end, let us cease all conversation until we have journeyed to our destination and are safely within the confines of Brown Snake Inlet. To do otherwise would be most foolhardy.

"Come, we must away. All those who dwell in Brown Snake Inlet eagerly await your arrival, Master Clayton."

"'Tis truly so," agreed Tallulah, nodding her head shyly, her large blue eyes half- hidden beneath her long, fluttering eyelashes.

"A firm grip is called for, young master," Mortimer instructed. "Our sally forth into the depths shall be brief, but, I assure you, most rapid." Then winding his tail into a tight coil and using it like a spring, Mortimer pushed hard against the rocky edge of the Reflective Reef, and shot out into the water. The sudden burst of speed flung Clayton forward; only his tight grip around Mortimer's body prevented him from falling off.

With Tallulah by his side, Mortimer turned south and began the journey to Brown Snake Inlet.

Chapter 11

Brown Snake Inlet

As soon as Mortimer and Tallulah reached the end of the Reflective Reef, they headed due east, swimming against the force of the green water Travel Current.

They swam single file, each taking turns leading the way. Clayton noticed that the snakes were drafting off each other, like bicyclists do when they ride in groups. The lead snake cut through the wind and current, pulling the rear snake along its wake. Whoever was in front waved his tail when he was ready to switch places and rest.

Soon land came into view, and the snakes veered south again. They swam on, hugging the shoreline, one behind the other. In some places, the forest rose up in a gradual slope, in others in a much steeper incline. And everywhere, the trees grew almost to the water's edge, separated from it only by a narrow, rocky beach covered with thousands of purple stones.

When they reached Brown Snake Inlet, Mortimer and Tallulah swam through its narrow entrance, past caves and tributaries until they reached a stone archway, which spanned the opening to a large, vaulted cave. Swimming side by side, they entered.

"'Tis to this destination, Brown Snake Meeting Hall, that we three have journeyed forth from the Reflective Reef," said Mortimer, breaking his long silence. "I beg your indulgence, Master Clayton. It is necessary that you now dismount. Kindly rest upon this rock whilst I take leave to summon together our assembly," he continued, pointing his tail to a large, flat rock just above the water's edge. "Tallulah shall remain ever by your side."

Clayton slid off Mortimer's back into the water and hoisted himself up onto the rock. From his vantage point, he could see the entire interior of the cave. Sunlight streamed through the stone archway bouncing off the smooth, white stone walls and vaulted ceiling. A cool, fresh breeze, smelling faintly of the sea, wafted through the air.

He picked up a flat stone lying by his feet and skipped it across the surface of the water. "*PLUNK! PLUNK! PLUNK!*" The sound of the pebble's three skips filled the cave.

"That was loud!"

"Pardon?" Tallulah's voice rang out.

"Your voice, and the skipping stone, the sounds are so loud and clear. They sound like they're coming from all directions at once; like when you're wearing headphones, or hearing surround sound in a movie theater."

"All sounds here are thus. 'Tis the consequence of this meeting hall. Sound here travels clear and true, like a bell.

The faintest of whispers can be heard by all."

No sooner had Tallulah finished speaking, then a "*SSSSSH*" sounded throughout the cave. A procession of 14 large brown snakes led by Mortimer entered Brown Snake Meeting Hall and swam towards them. They arranged themselves around Mortimer—three on his left, and the remaining ten in two rows of five, on his right.

Mortimer began to speak.

Chapter 12
Brown Snake Meeting Hall

"On behalf of myself, my beloved Tallulah, and all assembled here, I bid you a most heartfelt welcome, Master Clayton," said Mortimer.

"Please allow me to introduce the esteemed representatives of the ten clans of Brown Snake Inlet," he continued, turning his head to the left, "Archibald, Clarissa, Ezra, Mildred, Jeremiah in front, and Priscilla, Maximilian, Rebecca, Wallace, and Victoria behind. And, to my right, our three revered Scribes: Lady Abigail, Timothy the Elder, and Simon."

"Hello," said Clayton, looking down at the brown snakes assembled in the water below. "Hi. Nice to meet you."

"Greetings, Master Clayton," the snakes replied in unison, waving their tails from side to side in welcome. "We are delighted to at last make your acquaintance."

"We are forever indebted to you for your most expeditious response to our plea for assistance," said Mortimer. "I am certain that I speak for all who are gathered here when I express our deep regret regarding the unexpected curtailment of Miss Annie. It is our fervent hope that, in the not too distant future, we shall have the pleasure to also bid her welcome here.

"As you are no doubt aware, the ways of the Disruptors have drastically altered of late. No longer are they merely content with mischievous deeds. 'Tis my belief that the malfunction to the Travel Current is yet more evidence of their darkening transgressions."

"Your message said there was trouble with The Scrolls," said Clayton. "What have the Disruptors done to them?"

"Now that we are within the safety and privacy of Brown Snake Meeting Hall, I am at last at liberty to recount the dire happenings that have befallen The Scrolls. However, I must first render a brief explanation regarding their unique and essential nature.

"The Scrolls of Tilania have existed since the beginning of recorded time. Upon them are written all that is known of the past, present, and future of Tilania and the Underworld."

"Who gets to use them?"

"No one."

"You mean no one ever reads them?"

"That is correct Master Clayton. Once written upon, The Scrolls are never looked on again. Their sole purpose is but to exist, untouched and undisturbed forever. It is their everlasting presence that makes possible the balance and harmony of Tilania and the Underworld. Since time immemorial, the Scribes of Brown Snake Inlet have served as the keepers and protectors of The Scrolls. Should The Scrolls ever be examined after they are written on by the Scribes, chaos and destruction surely would follow."

"I don't get it. Don't the Scribes know what is written on them?"

"No, Master Clayton. Once they depart the Portal of Time, the Scribes can no longer recall what they have written. Such is the power of the waters surrounding the Portal of Time that forgetfulness is imparted unto all who journey there[4]. All that remains in memory is an enduring sense of calm and well-being."

"Portal of Time? What is that?"

"The Portal of Time is the passageway a Scribe must traverse to gain entry into the Inner Chamber wherein The Scrolls reside. On the 11th day of each month, at the second 11th hour, all three Scribes meet here, in Brown Snake Meeting Hall, to venture forth to the Portal of Time," Mortimer explained, gesturing with his tail to a dark opening beneath the rocks. "Only one Scribe is allowed entry. The means by which a Scribe is chosen remains forever unknown. Once inside the chamber, it is the task of the chosen Scribe, in the time allotted, to unfurl The Scrolls, and record therein all that shall come to pass in Tilania and the Underworld from thence until the next date of entry. This done, at the stroke of midnight, no sooner and no

---

[4] *In Greek mythology, the Lethe is one of the five rivers in Hades. It was believed that anyone who drank from the Lethe forgot everything he or she knew. In Tilania's Underworld, the Scribe who swam through the Portal of Time's waters forgot everything he or she knew of The Scrolls and the Inner Chamber.*

later, the Scribe must depart and return to Brown Snake Meeting Hall.

"Alas, of late, a most unthinkable catastrophe has occurred. The Disruptors, we know not how, have gained entry through the Portal of Time and have disturbed The Scrolls."

"They got in?" Clayton gasped.

"That this be so, we have no doubt. Indeed the Disruptors have wrought a deed so heinous, so malicious, that all who dwell in Tilania and the Underworld are in mortal danger. The future is now at risk of collapse. A great tragedy has befallen us."

Chapter 13

The Fragment

"Wait a sec," said Clayton. "How do you know anything is wrong? If the water around the Portal of Time makes the Scribes forget everything, how do they did know that The Scrolls were disturbed?"

"A most astute inquiry, Master Clayton," said Mortimer. "However, Lady Abigail, the second-last to be granted entry," he continued, pointing to the slightly smaller, brown snake nearest him, her scales decorated with small interlocking orange colored circles, "exited the Portal of Time with a premonition of doom, rather than the customary enduring sense of calm and well-being. Such a happening had never before occurred."

"You mean like after a bad dream? When you wake up and you can't remember anything. All you have is an awful feeling," asked Clayton.

"Exactly so," said Mortimer, nodding solemnly. "As a consequence of this strange occurrence, with no further delay, an emergency assembly was called. Representatives from all ten clans of Brown Snake Inlet—those now assembled before you—partook of a long and arduous deliberation. Presently, it was decreed that the Scribe next granted entry would deviate from the prescribed protocol. Not only would the Scribe write upon The Scrolls, as is our custom, but, for the first time ever, record upon a sheet of waterproof vellum, all that he or she witnessed within those hallowed surrounds. In this way would we discover what, if anything, had befallen The Scrolls.

"Alas," Mortimer continued, gesturing to the snake next to Abigail, "Simon, the chosen Scribe, emerged with the same sense of dread. Moreover, when he returned to all gathered here, uncurled his tail, and released the vellum sheet, we beheld, much to our horror, inscribed upon it, the unmistakable star-shaped mark of the Disruptors!

"Worst still, upon the sheet of vellum lay a disintegrating fragment of The Scrolls themselves. Such is the unique nature of The Scrolls' parchment that it endureth forever. That it should be found thus is incomprehensible.

"But a more grievous calamity was yet to follow. Whilst our learned elders diligently sought to ascertain the cause of this catastrophe, the fragment disappeared. In its place was left, once again, the star-shaped imprint of the Disruptors.

"It was at that instant that I was dispatched to Tilania, that I might elicit Kalya's help in summoning both you and your companion, Miss Annie, that you might assist us in our dire plight."

With Tallulah by his side, Clayton studied the solemn faces of the snakes gathered before him: to his left, the representatives of the ten clans, in two rows of five, to his right, the three Scribes, and, directly in front, Mortimer.

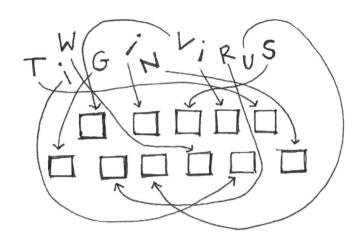

Chapter 14

Twig in Virus

Annie climbed out of the drafty Passageway into the cave, its darkness instantly illuminated by her Nocto-Vision. Once outside, she switched it off, found her duffel bag, changed out of her suit, and ran to the rowboat. She rowed as fast as she could toward the strange, spherical hull of The Jenny N anchored in the distance. She kept thinking about Thila Mae's anagrammed message for Kalya. "Twig in virus" meant "visit Gruwin"; but what was in the Forest of Gruwin?

When Annie was a few yards from the boat she let out a gasp. That's it!, she thought. Thila Mae was telling them that the Disruptors were in the Forest of Gruwin!

She stopped, secured her oars, and dropped anchor. Then she clapped her hands together twice, the way Mr. Ness had done the first time she and Clayton had boarded The Jenny N.

The boat's entry system activated. The hatch door at the top of the sphere opened and a rope ladder appeared, and unwound itself down the side of the boat. When it reached the water, it transformed into a thin, translucent walkway that skimmed along the water's surface, coming to rest next to the rowboat. Annie stepped onto the walkway, and made her way towards the boat, the walkway bouncing and swaying with the weight of each step. Once she reached the rope ladder, she climbed to the hatch door, entered the boat, and descended the circular staircase into the center of the cabin.

"Annie, what are you doing here?" asked Kalya, swiveling his captain's chair towards her. "Why are you back so soon? Where's Clayton?" he asked, glancing over Annie's shoulder with a puzzled look on his face.

"He's still in the Underworld. I couldn't get on the Travel Current so I came back. It stopped working right after Clayton got on. This weird big bird, Thila Mae, came to fix it. She told me you were old friends."

"That's right, we are. Thila Mae is the technician, or mechanic, for the air Travel Currents in the Underworld. Her twin brother, Max, is the technician for the water Travel Currents."

Kalya turned his chair back towards the instrument panel, repositioned his shell, and gestured to Annie to sit down. She sat cross-legged on the floor beside him, her back to the cluttered living area, Mr. Ness's laboratory to her right. Nothing in the lab had changed. The shelves were still stuffed full of three-dimensional models and half-finished projects. The large tabletop was still littered with Mr. Ness's itty-bitty robots, some lying down, others sitting propped up against one another.

"I don't know Max well, but I've worked with Thila Mae many times," Kalya continued. "She can fix just about anything. I called on her once to help our team when we were rebuilding Keriam. One look at Mr. Ness's plans and she had the problem figured out. The synchronizer on the Rock Timer was malfunctioning. Then she fixed it—something we had been trying to do for weeks! I still have no idea how she did it. All I know is she never stopped talking or doing things that didn't make sense. But when she finished whatever it was she was doing, the synchronizer on the Rock Timer started working perfectly."

"That's exactly what happened when the Travel Current broke. She kept jabbering away, telling me stuff I couldn't understand, and doing one weird thing after another. She even got me to help her. I was sure the Travel Current was never going to be repaired. But she fixed it. I couldn't believe it! I didn't think she would; that's why I told Clayton to go on without me and came back here."

Kalya's eyes opened wide and he let out a gasp. "You sent Clayton a message?"

"Don't worry, I sent it in Morse code to make sure the Disruptors wouldn't be able to read it. But, even if they did read it, they already knew the Travel Current was broken. They're the ones who did it. Thila Mae showed me their star-shaped mark in the sand right beside the Indicator Rocks."

"The Disruptors vandalized the Travel Currents?" Kalya asked, rubbing his face with his left front tentacle, a look of concern in his eyes.

"Yes, and there is something else. When I told Thila Mae I was going back to The Jenny N to see you, she said, 'Tell 'em, twig in virus. Got that? Twig in virus. Don't you forget.'"

"Twig in virus?' I wonder what she meant by that."

"I figured it out. You know how she loves anagrams, like her name: Thila Mae Technician is 'The Tilania Mechanic'... well, 'twig in virus' is an anagram too. When you rearrange the letters you get 'visit Gruwin.' Thila Mae must know that Clayton and I are here because of the Disruptors. I think she's trying to help us. She's telling us where to find them."

"You might be onto something, Annie. Take a look at this." Kalya reached over and pressed the green button to illuminate the screen above the instrument panel. The cabin's interior darkened and a large map of Tilania appeared. Kalya pointed to Tondore Island, southeast of Nessen. The Forest of Gruwin, its boundaries outlined with small blue blinking lights, occupied almost the entire eastern half of the island. A red line, marking the course of The Wide River from its beginning on the western side, wound its way through the central valley and into Five-Sided Lake in the Forest of Gruwin.

"These orange dots show all the places the Disruptors have left their star-shaped imprint. Over the course of a typical year, we find a total of 10 to 15 such marks in Tilania and the Underworld combined. But in the past month alone, 20 new marks have been found, all in the Forest of Gruwin!" Kalya said, as he turned a large dial on the instrument panel to magnify the mapped image.

"This close up of the Forest of Gruwin shows exactly where the marks were discovered," he continued, gesturing to the screen. "Thila Mae is right. We need to 'visit Gruwin' to find the Disruptors."

"But the Forest of Gruwin looks huge," said Annie, examining the map. "And there are dots everywhere. How do we decide where to go first?"

"Solano Bay is on the northwest side of Tondore Island," said Kalya, pointing to the map with a tentacle. He turned the dial on the instrument panel once again. A close-up of Solano Bay and the edge of the Forest of Gruwin appeared. "Here's where the trail begins. It's about three miles to the edge of the Forest of Gruwin."

"Look, there is an orange dot right where the forest starts," Annie said, standing up and gesturing to the map.

"Yes. The trail should pass right by it. I'll download all this data onto our MRVDs," Kalya said.

"This map has so much detail about Tondore Island, did Mr. Ness go there?" Annie asked.

"Yes, more than once in fact. He wrote about his visits in those notebooks over there," said Kalya, pointing to the cluttered bookshelf to his left.

"Have you been there too?"

"No, but I always wanted to go."

"Thila Mae said she went there."

"No, I'm sure Thila Mae has never been to Tondore Island. She has been on The Jenny N, but like most Underworldians, except me of course, she doesn't like to travel."

"But she has. She knows all about the Forest of Gruwin."

"I assure you, all she knows she learned from her studies at the Reflective Reef."

"But I know she was there," insisted Annie.

"How can you be so sure?"

"She told me that's where she got a spare Bit Joiner, whatever that is. And she also said it was a nice place, except for the bad bugs."

"That sounds just like Thila Mae," said Kalya, a hint of a chuckle in his voice. "She chatters on, but most of the time it doesn't mean a thing."

"It really sounded like she had been there," Annie persisted.

"I have to admit, you never can tell when it comes to Thila Mae. She's always full of surprises."

....

Kalya set the coordinates on the instrument panel for Tondore Island, and pulled the lever. There was a deep rumbling as the ship's anchor began reeling itself in. When it clunked into place in its stowage area, Kalya plugged in the coordinates for Solano Bay, engaged the thrusters and the boat began its journey to Tondore Island.

This was Kalya's first voyage as captain of The Jenny N. The closest he had come to skippering a boat was a simulated sea voyage he took in a navigational class many years before, when he was a student at the Reflective Reef Institute of Learning.

Chapter 15

Emergency!

The assembly of brown snakes remained motionless, their eyes fixed on Clayton. The only sound in the cave was of waves lapping against its stone walls. The stillness and silence made Clayton uncomfortable. He began to fidget. To his relief, Mortimer began to speak once again.

"We must endeavor to reclaim the missing fragment of The Scrolls. Only then may we begin to discover the affliction from which it now suffers, and thus devise a remedy. Should we fail in our efforts to render The Scrolls complete once more, ruin and destruction will surely befall all who dwell in Tilania and the Underworld."

"We should set a trap to catch them," Clayton said.

"No, Master Clayton. It is our firm conviction that the Disruptors shall not return. The Scrolls are but a part of a sinister plot to…"

At that moment, Clayton's MRVD sounded three loud beeps. He unzipped the pocket on the front of his suit, retrieved his MRVD, and saw the words "voice message" blinking on the screen. He turned on the speaker and heard a voice whisper, "*Psst. Psst.* Emergency! Emergency! Come immediately!"

It was Mr. Ness!

It seemed strange to Clayton that Mr. Ness's message was not in Morse code.

As soon as the message finished, Mr. Ness's whispering voice began again. "Psst. Psst. Emergency! Emergency! Come immediately!" resonated through the meeting hall.

Clayton jumped up, and in his excitement almost knocked his MRVD into the water.

"It's a message from Mr. Ness. I've got to go to home now!"

"Indeed, you must," replied Mortimer. "Perchance the cause of your hasty departure shall prove advantageous to our most dire circumstance.

"Come, my lad, let us hasten to the Reflective Reef. I trust that, if all is as it should be, the Travel Current is no longer impaired and may now transport you homeward."

Clayton climbed onto Mortimer's back and they exited the meeting hall through the arched entry, and swam the length of the narrow inlet out into the open sea. When they came to a large outcropping of rocks, Mortimer stopped and wound his tail in a tight coil.

"Hold firm, Master Clayton," he said, pushing his tail hard against the surface of the rock. The force of the unwinding coil flung them forward, far out to sea.

"Our journey northward to the Reflective Reef will prove most rapid, I assure you. For unlike our journey thence, we now travel in the direction of the powerful green Water Current. We shall take full advantage of this propitious circumstance and allow it to propel us swiftly forward."

Chapter 16

The Return to Earth

"The time has come to bid you farewell, Master Clayton," said Mortimer when they reached the Reflective Reef. "Return to us soon. I trust you shall convey the particulars of our plight to Mr. Ness. 'Tis my belief that he has summoned you homeward for a purpose of paramount import, one that shall prove pertinent to our cause."

"Yeah, Mr. Ness must know something important that will help," said Clayton, sliding off Mortimer's back and scrambling onto the Reflective Reef. "I'll be back as soon as I can."

"I bid you farewell," said Mortimer. "May your journey home be expeditious." Then he turned and swam away, his long tail swaying a goodbye.

Clayton did not bother to check if the Travel Current was working again. He had decided not to use it. Instead, he was going to try to return home using Travel by Desire.[5] If it worked, it would be faster than anything else. Annie had used it to travel from Tilania back to Earth when she was chasing Dennis. She said that each time the whole trip was over in a few seconds. But this was different—traveling between the Underworld and Earth was untested. Mr. Ness had always said that there was too much interference for it to work, but Clayton was determined to give it a try anyway.

He closed his eyes and concentrated, picturing the inside of Mr. Ness's workshop and the old wooden stool with the wobbly leg. He waited. His left eyelid started to twitch. His ears began to ring. He couldn't tell if the travel method was working. He wondered if and when he should open his eyes. Finally, unable to resist, he looked.

Travel by Desire had worked! He was back on Earth, standing in the middle of Mr. Ness's workshop wearing his regular clothes. But Mr. Ness wasn't there!

"Clayton, where are you?" he heard his dad call out. "Annie is already in the car." His dad's footsteps grew louder and louder. Then they stopped, and the workshop door swung open. "There you are. Didn't you hear me? Come on, let's go."

Clayton hesitated. He wasn't sure what was happening. Then he remembered what Annie had told him about traveling from one world to another; sometimes it caused unintended time travel. When Annie and Kalya traveled to Earth from Tilania to stop Dennis, they arrived three days earlier then when she had first left. It was tricky. She had

---

[5] *Travel by Desire, part of The Ness Theory, is based on the principle that desire can provide the fuel and means for travel.*

to remember to relive things exactly the same way she had the first time so that nothing in the future would be affected.

Clayton wondered if the same thing had happened to him too. Had he traveled through time? Was he in the past or was he in the future? He would have to be careful how he acted.

"Coming…I can't find my backpack," Clayton heard himself say to his dad. He hadn't planned on saying anything more, but his mouth opened, and words came tumbling out. It felt as if someone else was doing the talking. "I thought I left it in the front hall."

There was something eerily familiar about the way his dad pointed under Mr. Ness's workbench, shook his head, and said, "No wonder you couldn't find it. There it is, shoved in the corner."

Clayton vaguely remembered his dad coming to fetch him in the workshop and finding his backpack. He knew it had happened a few days before Kalya had sent his mirror-written message, but he wasn't sure exactly when. He followed his dad to the car, not saying a word for fear of messing up the future by mentioning things that hadn't happened yet. He climbed into the backseat next to Annie, hoping she'd say or do something that would give him a clue as to what day it was, but she just smiled and went back to reading her book.

"I just ran into Ms. Warren at the grocery store," Clayton's dad said, as he pulled out of the driveway. "She asked me how your science project was coming along."

Clayton shifted nervously in his seat. Now he knew exactly what day it was. He remembered this conversation all too clearly. It had happened one week before Kalya's message.

"I didn't tell her it was the first I'd heard about a science project," his dad went on, gripping the steering wheel tightly with both hands. "She said it was assigned at the beginning of March and is due a week from Friday. Please tell me you've been working on it and haven't left everything until the last minute."

"I'll get it done, Dad. Honest. No problem."

Clayton felt even worse than the first time he had this conversation. His last minute approach to homework drove his dad crazy. He had a topic picked out already, which, for him, was actually quite impressive. He usually procrastinated for so long he ended up doing everything the night before. The worst part about being in this particular situation was that he knew what was going to happen next. He would find the instructions that he had misplaced, but nothing else would get done on his science project this week. There was a distinct disadvantage of time travel. Nothing could be done to change what was about to happen. He would have to let the week unfold the same way it had the first time, otherwise he could mess up the future and his trip back to Tilania.

Annie looked up from her book and winked at him, as if they were sharing a secret. For a moment, Clayton thought she was winking about his travel back in time or about Kalya's message. But then he remembered there was no way she could know about either of these things. They hadn't happened yet!

He stared out the car window and concentrated on making a mental list of all the things he needed to remember to do when they found Kalya's message a week from now:

1) Be surprised when Mr. Ness shows them that the message is in mirror writing.

2) Pretend not to know that the brown snake's name is Mortimer, or that he has a wife named Tallulah.

3) Remember not to say anything about the Portal of Time, the Disruptors, or the disintegrating fragment of The Scrolls.

As Clayton's dad pulled into their driveway, Annie closed her book, leaned over and whispered to Clayton, "If you need the instructions for the science project, just call me after dinner." Then in a much louder voice she said, "Thanks for the ride Mr. Irving." She waved back at Clayton and his dad as she crossed their backyard, opened the back gate, and headed toward her back door.

"Bye Annie," Clayton's dad called back, lifting his briefcase off the front seat and getting out of the car. He turned and peered into the back seat through his open car door. "What's going on with you Clayton?" he asked. "Why don't you stop daydreaming and come on inside."

Chapter 17

A Discovery

Clayton grabbed his backpack, got out of the car, and headed into the house. He helped his dad unload the dishwasher, refilled Prince's water bowl, and washed his hands for dinner. It felt strange to be doing and saying the same things he had done and said before—like a programmed robot. But it wasn't exactly the same. This time, while he was reliving all the things he had done before, he was also thinking about Mortimer, the fate of The Scrolls, and Annie's whereabouts in Tilania.

After dinner, he went to his room and rummaged through his backpack, looking for the science project instructions. His memory was so poor he couldn't remember where he had found them the first time. They weren't in the folder marked Science Project, or in any other folder. He did find the math homework he had forgotten to turn in that morning, as well as a crumpled up five dollar bill he had saved to buy a snack before his soccer practice last Monday.

He was about to call Annie, when he remembered where he had put the instructions. They were inside the front cover of the book he checked out of the school library. The title of the book was *The Aurora Borealis, Legends and Facts*. Aurora Borealis was the proper name for the northern lights.

Clayton's mom had told him that she had seen the northern lights (that's what she always called them) when she was a girl. They lit up the night sky, spreading across it like a giant curtain that shimmered and shook in the wind. Sometimes they were greenish blue, and other times reddish purple.

He was excited to read about the northern lights again. Especially the different legends that explained what they were. The Native American Fox Tribe believed they were the ghosts of enemies they had killed who were restless and searching for revenge. Other Native Americans said they were human spirits dancing. The Labrador Inuit thought they were torches in the sky lit by the spirits to show the dead the way to heaven.

Clayton's mom told him that she liked pretending the northern lights were whispering secrets to her in a special language only she could understand.

Clayton remembered asking his mom if he could stay up late so he could see them too and hear them whispering. But she explained that you couldn't see the northern lights in the Oakville sky. She said you had to be somewhere close to the North Pole, someplace like Siberia or Greenland, or the northern part of Canada where she was from.

Clayton liked remembering his mom, especially at night when he was going to sleep. But sometimes thinking about her made him feel lonely. And sad, deep inside. She had died in a car accident a week after his seventh birthday.

....

There was only one person absent on Friday morning when Ms. Warren took attendance—Dennis. He was at a memorial service for his uncle who had disappeared while on a scientific expedition in the fall. His family had just learned that he had been killed in an accident. Ms. Warren passed around a card for everyone to sign. It was a picture of a setting sun with a black border around it. Inside it said, "Those who have perished live on in our hearts."

Clayton felt sad that someone had died, but he didn't feel bad for Dennis. In fact, he was thrilled that Dennis was absent from class. Clayton despised him. He was a bully. He was the kind of kid who was always trying to get other kids in trouble. He snitched on them any chance he got, and snooped around trying to find out things that weren't any of his business. Last fall he tried to steal the stamp with the red rowboat that Clayton and Annie used to travel to Tilania. Luckily, Annie received a warning from the Reflective Reef and she and Kalya figured out a way to stop him.

Clayton opened the card. It was filled with his classmates' signatures. He was pretending to add his own, when he noticed Ms. Warren's note at the top. He hadn't bothered to read it the first time all this happened. Without meaning to, he let out a gasp.

"Dennis," it read, "Our deepest sympathy for the loss of your uncle, Professor Franco Dismali."

Franco Dismali! Clayton couldn't believe it. Dennis's uncle was Mr. Ness's old lab partner, Franco Dismali! The same Franco Dismali who had travelled to Tilania, kidnapped Mr. Ness, and forced him to build the weather machine on the Isle of Hearts.

It made sense. Franco didn't die in an accident while on a scientific expedition on Earth. He was killed on the Isle of Hearts, during his secret trip to Tilania. No one but Clayton, Annie, Kalya, Ralph and Mr. Ness knew this. It was true Franco's death was an accident. It happened when he left the safety of the school building during the earthquake and ran back to the lab to steal the weather machine. He was crushed by a falling tree. The exact one Clayton and Annie had helped Ralph weaken by sawing through part of it. They only intended to destroy the weather machine, but Franco got in the way. He wanted the weather machine so he could use it to control Earth.

Like most criminals, Franco's greed overshadowed his judgment and led directly to his demise.

But, there were still many unanswered questions. Had Franco used Dennis to spy on Clayton and Annie while they were building the microscope in Mr. Ness's workshop? Was that how Franco found out Mr. Ness was in Tilania? Did Dennis know his uncle hadn't died in an accident on Earth? Did he think he was still alive?

Chapter 18
Autopilot

"Clayton, why aren't you outside? The bell rang five minutes ago," Ms. Warren said, straightening the papers on her desk and standing up to leave.

Clayton looked around the empty classroom. Everyone was at recess. Clayton…the bell rang five minutes ago. That was exactly what Ms. Warren had said to him the first time. Reliving life was weird. It didn't matter what he was thinking about, everything was happening the same way it had happened before.

Clayton stood up and started walking towards the door. It felt strange, like he was a puppet on a string and someone else was controlling how he moved and what he said. He realized there was an advantage to having his body and voice on autopilot. It left his mind free to think about Dennis and Franco while the rest of him continued to relive the day.

It made sense to Clayton that Franco was Dennis's uncle. That explained why Dennis knew so much about Mr. Ness. Mr. Ness had mysteriously disappeared ten and a half years before, right after Franco stole the blueprints for the weather machine. Franco could not build the weather machine alone. He needed Mr. Ness. He must have been searching for him all of those years and keeping an eye on his workshop in case he ever came back. So he knew about Clayton and Annie and that they went to Aunt Jenny's house after school everyday. He couldn't risk being seen near the house because he was under suspicion for Mr. Ness's disappearance. That's why he had Dennis spy on Clayton and Annie. It was a smart plan. If Dennis got caught, it would be no big deal. He would just be a kid playing a prank. Dennis always got into trouble; no one would ever suspect someone had put him up to it.

Since Dennis was spying on them, he knew when they started putting the microscope together. But why had Dennis tried to steal the red rowboat stamp? Franco didn't need it, he had figured out his own way of getting to Tilania. In fact, Franco must have never known about the stamp at all, otherwise, he would have been on the lookout for Clayton and Annie in Tilania and would have suspected that they would help Mr. Ness.

On Friday night, Clayton packed for the over night camping trip he was taking with his dad. In the morning they headed to Leliac Falls, an hour's drive away. He loved camping there. For the first time since he started "reliving" his week, he enjoyed himself. He and his dad hiked, swam in the river beneath the waterfalls, roasted hotdogs and made s'mores over the campfire. Clayton's dad didn't say much. He never did. But that was fine with Clayton, he had plenty to think about.

He was certain that Franco knew another way to get to Tilania. And, in order to set the trap for Mr. Ness and hypnotize him, he must have been to Tilania more than once. He wondered if Franco's travels to Tilania were related to The Scrolls's disintegration.

As they were breaking camp in the morning, Clayton sensed someone or something watching him. He heard soft crunching noises and looked over his shoulder. He saw a little brown squirrel spinning a nut in his claws in that nervous way squirrels do. Then, like the first time he lived this trip, Clayton accidentally dropped the tent rod he was holding and the startled  squirrel ran away, dropping his half-eaten nut. But this time Clayton got a better look at it. At first he thought it was an acorn. It sure looked like one. It had the same funny little pointed cap. But, it wasn't brown, it was purple.

"Are you ready to roll up the tent?" Clayton's dad asked, bringing Clayton's study of the nut to an end.

"Yeah," Clayton answered. Kneeling on the tarp next to the collapsed tent, he picked up the dropped rod and put it in the bag with the others.

After they finished packing the car with their belongings, they doused the campfire with water and started the drive home.

Clayton knew he had to be patient and use this time to watch, think, and learn anything he could about Dennis and Franco, and whether or not they had a role in the disintegration of The Scrolls. But, what he wanted more than anything was to skip ahead to Thursday. Then he would finally find out why Mr. Ness had sent him the urgent message and whether he knew that Dennis was Franco's nephew.

As expected, it was raining on Monday morning when Clayton woke up.

"You almost ready?" Clayton's dad shouted from the bottom of the stairs.

"Darn. I forgot to set my alarm again," Clayton muttered, shaking himself awake. "Be down in a minute," he shouted back.

"What's taking so long?"

"I'm getting my stuff for soccer."

It was too late to catch the bus, so his dad had to drive him to school. Clayton was glad. He didn't want to be on the bus with Annie. It would be too hard to resist telling her about Dennis and the disintegrating Scrolls. Clayton wouldn't be tempted to talk to her at school. He couldn't risk it; there were too many kids around. At recess he headed outside and saw something he hadn't noticed before. Dennis was at the far end of the playground surrounded by a group of kids. That was strange, Dennis was usually alone. Clayton couldn't hear what anyone was saying, but he could see that Dennis was showing them something. Whatever it was, it was small enough to fit in the palm of Dennis's hand, but Clayton was too far away to figure out what it was.

The bell rang. Everyone went back inside. Dennis sat down at his seat next to Clayton, and unzipped his backpack. As he reached inside for his science textbook, a black notebook tumbled out. He shoved it back inside, but not before Clayton saw the initials "F.D." written on the cover.

"It's time to talk about your science projects," Ms. Warren said. "When I call your name, please stand up and tell us the topic you're investigating. Let's start with table one."

Clayton's seat was at table six; it would be the last table to be called. Student after student rose and gave a brief description of their project. But Clayton didn't hear anyone. He was too busy thinking about the initials "F.D." on the cover of Dennis's black notebook. A cold shiver shot up Clayton's spine. Franco Dismali. Of course! That was it. "F.D." stood for Franco Dismali.

The sound of Dennis's voice startled him to attention.

"Ah, yeah. I'm trying to grow two plants," Dennis explained.

"Hmm, that's interesting. But why is that worthy of study?" Ms. Warren asked.

"Ah, um, I'm trying to see what happens to two seedlings. I left one growing in the sun and put the other one in the dark."

"Aside from exposure to light, will their growing conditions continue to be the same?"

"Yeah," Dennis answered. "The two pots have the same soil and um, I'm watering them the same amount."

"So, class, can you help Dennis with his hypothesis?" asked Ms. Warren looking around the room. "Yes, Annie."

"Plants need sun to grow,[6]" Annie said, her voice beginning to tremble. Clayton could see Dennis glowering at her. "Sun provides the energy for photosynthesis to occur," Annie added, her voice trailing off into little more than a whisper.

"Yes! Very good," Ms. Warren smiled. She turned back to Dennis. "What type of plants are you growing?"

Dennis looked down and started to fidget with a button on his shirt. "I don't know," he said. He pulled a large purple seed out of his pocket. "This is what they look like." Clayton could see that the seed had a little capped top. It looked like the nut he had seen the squirrel eating when he was on his camping trip.

"How unusual," said Ms. Warren. "It looks like a purple colored acorn. Where did you find it?"

"My uncle gave them to me," Dennis answered nervously, shoving the seed back in his pocket.

"I see. I read that botany was one of his hobbies. He collected and grew unusual plants from all over the world. People sent him rare species to identify. Where did he tell you those were from?" Ms. Warren asked.

"He didn't. He just gave them to me," Dennis answered as he sat down.

Clayton realized that the purple seeds were what Dennis had been showing the kids at recess. His heart

....

[6] *Parasitic plants do not need sunlight to live. Instead of using the sun's energy, carbon dioxide, and water to make their own food (photosynthesis) they live off the nutrients of their host plants. It is estimated that over 4000 parasitic plant species exist.*

skipped a beat. He had seen those purple seeds before! Thousands of them covered the shores of Brown Snake Inlet.

He couldn't prove it yet, but Clayton was sure there was a connection between Dennis, the purple seeds, and the disintegration of The Scrolls. He had to get a look at the notebook with "F.D." written on the front.

But how?

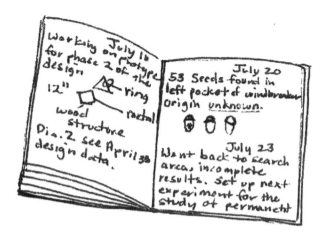

Chapter 19

Monday Again

At 2:55 PM, the dismissal bell rang. Clayton wanted to dash out the door and head full-speed for the school bus, but, he couldn't; his progress to the exit was controlled by what had happened before. His legs felt like they were made of lead, like he was trying to run through water in the shallow end of a swimming pool. He tried to lift his left leg high into the air, but it only reached forward and down to the ground with a regular step. Then his right leg took a step, then his left, and he walked with the other bus-kids right out the door, down the hall, and outside to wait for the school bus. Some kid was yelling to another, "Gross! You just sneezed on my jacket," as he got into line behind them. He felt a tap on his shoulder. "Your backpack?" he heard Annie say as she shoved his forgotten backpack into his arms. He felt his face break into a smile and the words, "Uh, thanks!" come out of his mouth.

Clayton wanted to be alone, away from his classmates, school, and even Annie. But he knew he didn't have a choice. He boarded the bus, sat down, opened his backpack, and tore out a piece of paper from his notebook. He folded it into a square. He didn't have scissors, so he carefully licked the top edge to weaken the paper and tore off the extra bit. After a few more folds, his paper creation was complete. "Football?" he asked, turning to Annie, but she shook her head no. He kneeled on his seat and looked behind him to the back of bus. He caught sight of Dennis two rows back. He couldn't see what he was doing.

Clayton tried to spy on him, but his body kept fidgeting, forcing him to look this way and that: out the window, in his lap, at the gash in the seatback in front of him. He poked his finger inside and wiggled it around. He absent-mindedly zipped and unzipped the front pocket of his backpack. Clayton then had a vague realization of what his teachers and his dad were always complaining about—he did indeed have trouble focusing.

"Goalpost?" Conrad called from the row directly behind him.

"Huh?"

"Goalpost. It's finished isn't it?"

"What, er…yeah," Clayton answered, as he turned backward to flick the football between Conrad's two outstretched index fingers.

"Score!" Clayton heard himself cheer.

"I'm up," Conrad said, retrieving the football from the empty seat beside him.

Clayton set up his index finger goal posts and waited for Conrad's football kick. His eyes looked up, past the ball toward Dennis.

"Switch seats, will ya?" Clayton asked.

"Why?" asked Conrad.

"Facing backward is making me feel sick."

Conrad gave Clayton a look of disapproval, but slid out of his row as Clayton climbed over the seat. Luckily, the bus driver didn't see.

"Feeling better now?" Conrad asked sarcastically, getting on his knees and turning to face Clayton.

"Go," Clayton said, ignoring the hard time Conrad was giving him.

"Set 'em up," Conrad answered.

As Clayton set up his goalposts, he remembered the errant shot Conrad was about to kick. Conrad aimed too high and the football flicked over Clayton's shoulder, landing on the floor at Dennis's feet.

"What was that?" Clayton asked, as he scrambled to get the ball. "Were you trying to flick it out the window?"

"Looking for something?" Dennis sneered, as he put the notebook he was studying down on the empty seat beside him. He leaned over and trapped the paper football under his foot.

Clayton didn't answer. He just stared at him. But as soon as Dennis bent over to get the football, Clayton sneaked a long look at the open pages of the notebook. He recognized the neat, legible handwriting. It was Franco's! There was a short entry dated July 20th. It read:

Fifty-three seeds found in left pocket of windbreaker. Origin unknown.

Underneath Franco's note there was a detailed colored sketch of three identical purple almond-shaped seeds, each with a little cap on top.

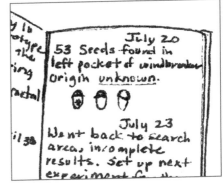

"Give it!" Clayton yelled, lunging at Dennis to grab the paper football the same way he had the first time it had happened. But this time, his eyes caught a glimpse of something on the drawing that took his breath away. One of the seeds had a star-shaped mark on it!

"Forget it. Let's go," Annie pleaded.

"What?" Clayton replied in a daze.

"It's no big deal," Annie said, shrugging her shoulders at Dennis who dangled the paper football just out of Clayton's reach.

"It's our stop. You can make another one later."

They crossed the street and climbed the steps to the Ness's house. "Hello Aunt Jenny," Clayton called to Mrs. Ness, as he hung his backpack next to Annie's in the front hall.

Annie and Clayton headed out the backdoor and to the workshop. The smell of gingersnaps wafting from the kitchen was a cruel reminder that it was only Monday. Clayton still had three more days to wait.

Chapter 20

Thursday at Last

The alarm clock blared a long, loud *BEEEEEEP.* Clayton woke up with a start. It was Thursday. He had finally made it. Waiting for the school day to end was torturous. He felt as if each minute was an hour and each hour a day. At last he was back in Mr. Ness's workshop with Annie. He sat on his stool, staring out the window.

Then it happened!

Ralph bolted out from under the workshop bench, almost knocking Annie off her stool.

"Clayton, look," yelled Annie, pushing her bangs out of her eyes. "There's a weird pattern in Ralph's fur!"

Clayton snapped to attention at the sound of Annie's long awaited words. He watched her sketch the pattern and heard himself say, "That shape…I've seen it before," as Mr. Ness left to get another cup of coffee.

He and Annie looked through the microscope at the stamp and discovered the message from Kalya. Mr. Ness returned to the workshop and flipped over the sheet of paper and held it up to the window. The decoded message read:

Trouble! Scrolls. Keepers can't! Suspicion, Disruptors! Assist POST-HASTE!!

Mr. Ness told them what he knew about the Disruptors, and Annie and Clayton got ready to jump into the stamp.

"Off you go," said Mr. Ness. Annie closed her eyes, counted to ten, and jumped.

But this time, instead of jumping after her, Clayton turned to Mr. Ness. "Finally," he exclaimed. "What happened? What is the emergency?"

"What are you talking about?" asked Mr. Ness, confused. "There is no emergency."

"Then why did you send that urgent message to my MRVD?" Clayton asked. "You said, 'come immediately,' so I did. But when I traveled back, I arrived a week earlier then the day we left. I have been reliving this whole week again and…"

"Slow down Clayton, start from the beginning," Mr. Ness interrupted, sitting down on his chair. "What message?"

Clayton stared at Mr. Ness in disbelief, blinking back tears of frustration. He had waited all this time, and now that he was finally able to ask Mr. Ness about his message, Mr. Ness had no idea what he was talking about.

Clayton took a deep breath and began again, "Annie and I went to Tilania, we found Kalya and he took us to the Passageway to the Underworld."

"Did Kalya get the Nocto-Vision working?" Mr. Ness asked, his eyes dancing with excitement.

"Herman," Clayton scolded, hearing himself use the same tone Aunt Jenny reserved for those times when she was especially frustrated with Mr. Ness.

"Sorry…very sorry," Mr. Ness apologized. "Please continue."

"I took the Travel Current to the Reflective Reef, but Annie couldn't get on. It stopped working. So she went back to Kalya and The Jenny N." Clayton patted his jean pockets, "Where is my MRVD? I have to tell her what's going on so she doesn't wait around for me. It must still be in my suit."

"The homing device on your MRVD prevents it from leaving Tilania. But don't worry, Annie won't notice you're gone."

"But I didn't jump!"

"True. But you jumped the first time and that is what has been recorded. As long as you jump in the next few hours, events will unfold exactly as they did the first time," Mr. Ness said, standing up and starting to pace. "Now, tell me what happened."

"Okay. I was with Mortimer, that's the brown snake's name, and fourteen other brown snakes in their meeting hall when I got a message on my MRVD. It was a voice recording. It sounded exactly like you!"

"What did it say?"

"It said, 'Psst. Psst. Emergency! Emergency! Come immediately!'"

Mr. Ness scratched his head. "Wha…."

"Wait, there's more," Clayton blurted out. "While I was reliving this week, I learned all this stuff about Dennis. He's Franco's nephew. Did you know that?"

Mr. Ness didn't answer. He stared ahead, his eyes alert and unsmiling.

"Dennis has always been spying on Annie and me. That's how he knew about the microscope and the stamp," Clayton's voice rose. "And, now he has Franco's seeds from the Underworld. They're same ones I saw on the shores of Brown Snake Inlet."

"Franco had seeds from the Underworld?"

"Yes. See, Dennis showed them to everyone at school. He must have stolen them from Franco's stuff, because he didn't know anything about them. He got nervous and started stammering when Ms. Warren asked him questions. Franco got them from the Disruptors."

"You know this for sure?"

"Yes, I'm positive. Dennis has Franco's notebook and I saw what Franco wrote inside. Franco said he found 53 seeds in the pocket of his windbreaker and he had drawings of three of them. One of the drawings had the Disruptor's star-shaped mark on it!"

"The Disruptor's mark?" Mr. Ness asked, the tips of his ears turning red. "What is Dennis doing with the seeds?"

"He's growing them for his science project."

"Hmmm. Franco said he had been to Tilania before. He went there looking for me." Mr. Ness said, starting to pace again. "When he found my hut and The Jenny N, he returned to Earth to make plans to kidnap me. That must be when the Disruptors put the seeds in his pocket."

"Okay, so he got the seeds then. But how did he meet the Disruptors? They have never been seen by any living thing."

"Tell me exactly what Franco wrote in his notebook."

"He wrote, '53 seeds found in left pocket of windbreaker. Origin unknown.'"

"The Disruptors must have slipped the dedian seeds into his pocket without his knowledge. Since they can't be seen, it would be easy for them to do. Franco didn't meet them. He probably didn't know they existed. The Disruptors knew Franco would bring the dedian seeds back to Earth. That is exactly what they wanted."

"What are dedian seeds?"

"Dedian seeds are the purple seeds you saw at Brown Snake Inlet. They're found throughout Tilania, too. The Scrolls are made from the paper harvested from the bark of dedian trees."

"I get it. Growing them on Earth must be causing the scroll paper to disintegrate," Clayton exclaimed.

"This can't continue," Mr. Ness agreed. "We must get those plants."

"The other weird thing is that I saw a squirrel eating a purple seed when I was camping. Do you think the squirrel was trying to help me?"

Chapter 21

Seeds and Plants

"You've got to get the dedian seeds and plants from Dennis," Mr. Ness insisted.

Clayton nodded in agreement, zipping up his sweatshirt and heading for the door.

"Be quick. Remember, you only have a few hours before you have to jump."

"Arf Arf!"

"What's that Ralph?" said Mr. Ness. "You want to go to Tilania?"

"Arf! Arf!" Ralph said again.

"You can't go. I need you here with me."

"Arf!"

"Ralph's got a point," Clayton interjected. "He should go to Tilania."

"Why?" Mr. Ness asked, a look of concern on his face.

"He can tell Annie why I'm still here."

"Good idea. Go ahead Ralph," Mr. Ness said, gesturing to the stamp that lay clamped on the microscope stage and rubbing at his face as if trying to erase its worried expression. "Remember the lessons Ralph," he added mysteriously. "They shouldn't be forgotten!"

"I'll see you on The Jenny N," said Clayton, rushing out the door.

"*Arf!*" Ralph answered, leaping into the stamp.

....

Dennis's house was only two blocks from the workshop. Clayton ran to the end of the block and turned right onto 15th Avenue. He crossed the street and turned into the alley that led to the back of Dennis's house. As he reached Dennis's back gate, he stumbled on something and lost his balance. He caught himself before he hit the pavement, his left ankle burning from twisting it. Biting his lip hard to stifle an ouch! he glanced down to see what he had tripped on. There was nothing on the ground except the garbage can and recycle bins that stood beside the gate. He heard a faint rustling of leaves overhead. Looking up, he saw a little brown squirrel perched motionless on the roof of Dennis's garage. It was the squirrel from the camping trip!

"Did you just trip me?" Clayton muttered under his breath.

The squirrel stared back at him, twitching his long bushy tail as if to answer.

"What am I thinking?" Clayton continued. "You can't talk."

The squirrel sat up on his hind legs and tilted his head, listening attentively.

Encouraged, Clayton began. "Where did you get that purple seed I saw you eating at Leliac Falls? Do you know where the rest of them are? Or the plants Dennis is growing?"

The squirrel twitched his tail again and scurried down the tree into Dennis's backyard.

Clayton gingerly opened the gate, hoping it wouldn't squeak, and slipped inside. He crept along, hugging the side of the fence and scanning the yard for the squirrel. He spotted him sitting on top of the garden shed. The squirrel looked straight at Clayton, twitched his tail, leapt onto the fence, and ran until it reached the side of Dennis's house. Then the squirrel stopped and looked back at Clayton with eager, expectant eyes.

As Clayton drew closer, he saw a purple plant in a terracotta pot. Its dark purple leaves were glossy and triangular shaped. It had already grown almost a foot high. Next to it stood an overturned wooden box.

Clayton was about to lift up the box when he heard a door creak open. He dashed behind the bushes that grew next to the fence.

"No way mom, I'm not going to," Dennis argued.

Clayton peered through the bushes and watched as

Dennis stomped out the side door, picked up his dirt bike that lay in the gravel next to the house, and pushed it through the backyard into the alley.

Clayton waited a few minutes, then left his hiding place and returned to the overturned box. He lifted it up. Underneath was the other dedian plant. Its leaves were wilted and its stalk limp from the lack of sunlight. He turned the box right side up and placed both plants inside.

"*Squeak! Squeak!*" the squirrel called out, as he ran back along the fence to the garden shed door.

"Oh, right. The seeds."

The squirrel twitched his tail in reply.

Clayton checked the windows that faced the backyard. All the blinds were pulled down. There was no sign of anyone. Staying close to the fence, he made his way to the garden shed and squeezed through the half-opened door.

The shed was filled with the musty smell of damp earth and stale air. Once his eyes adjusted to the dark, Clayton saw an assortment of garden tools hanging on the walls. A bag of planting soil sat on the ground and beside it an assortment of terracotta pots, stacked one on top of the another. Next to the pots was a bucket and inside the bucket, a small paper bag. Clayton peeked inside. It was filled with purple seeds.

He tucked the paper bag into his sweatshirt pocket, squeezed through the door, and crept back to the plants in the wooden box. He looked around again to make sure no one was watching. The blinds remained closed. He lifted up the wooden box containing the two plants and started back to the Ness's house.

He walked through the side yard to the workshop.

"Herman. Herman," Clayton shouted. "Open up."

Mr. Ness nodded to him through the workshop window and opened the door.

"Well done! Put the plants down over here," he said, shoving the messy stack of paper on his crowded workbench to one side.

"I got everything!" Clayton said, plopping down on the nearest stool. He reached inside his sweatshirt pocket and showed Mr. Ness the bag of seeds.

"Good work," Mr. Ness said, handing Clayton back the box with the two dedian plants. "Now off you go. Jump!"

Chapter 22
Pikdle Trees

The Jenny N's engines whirled with a droning hum as Annie and Kalya continued their journey to Tondore Island. "There is something strange about these Disruptor marks," said Kalya, examining the map.

"What do you mean?" Annie asked.

Kalya pointed to the orange dots scattered throughout the Forest of Gruwin. "The Disruptors left their marks, but there are no disruptions anywhere. When I got the data from the ship's computer, I thought it had malfunctioned, but I ran a complete diagnostic test and everything checks out. The Disruptors have left their marks, but nothing else."

"What do you mean there aren't any disruptions?"

"No mischief. No unusual changes. Nothing. Just their marks."

"Why would they do that?" she asked, brushing her bangs out of her eyes. "That doesn't make sense."

"I agree. It doesn't make sense."

"Maybe they're trying to throw us off track. You know, send us on a wild goose chase."

"What is a wild goose chase?" Kalya asked, confused.

"It's an idiom, a saying. It means looking in all the wrong places to find something. If someone sends you on a wild goose chase, they mislead you and trick you on purpose."

"Interesting. Maybe we need to start looking for something else in the Forest of Gruwin."

"Like what?"

"Maybe we can find a clue or pattern," Kalya answered, returning his attention to the detailed map of Tondore Island displayed on the ship's screen.

Annie leaned in closer to get a better look. She studied the terrain and the rivers, lakes, and streams for an answer. "Nothing looks unusual to me," she said, looking over at Kalya. Kalya's six tentacles were tucked into his shell and his green eyes were pensive.

"Let me try something," said Annie, turning away from the map and searching the workshop for a sheet of paper. When she found one, she folded it in half and then it in half again, and tore out a small piece from the folded corner. Next, she opened up the paper and held it at arm's length in front of her. She began to study the map through the dime-sized hole she had torn from its center, moving it slowly around the map.

"What are you doing?" Kalya asked.

"I learned this trick in drawing class. I thought it would be worth a try. Sometimes breaking things up into small pieces helps you understand the whole," Annie explained. "But I'm not seeing anything different. Here, you try."

Kalya extended his two front tentacles from inside his shell, took hold of the paper and studied the map. "I don't see anything either," he said, peering through the hole.

"What other details can you display on the map?" Annie asked.

"I'll add the flora overlay so we can take a closer look at the different species of plants, flowers, and trees," Kalya answered. He started tapping away at the instrument panel keyboard with his two front tentacles.

"You hunt and peck," Annie giggled. "Just like my grandfather."

"What?"

"On the keyboard. Like people who don't know how to type. They use one finger on each hand and search for every letter. When someone does that, it's called it 'hunt and peck' typing."

"This is how Fivskews are taught to use a keyboard," said Kalya, sounding a little defensive. "Of course, it works better when we use our screen glasses."

"What are those?"

"They are special glasses that reflect the keyboard upward. This slight modification to our field of vision increases our typing speed threefold. More importantly, it improves our 'connectivity ability.'"

"Your what?"

"Our eyes ability to discern patterns. Screen glasses enhance the Gestalt effect.[7] When you look through them, hidden patterns pop into view. Like when a connect-the-dots picture emerges."

"Why aren't you wearing them now?"

"I forgot they were fixed. They broke and Thila Mae repaired them. I was so busy the day she brought them back, I just stuck them in here and forgot about them," Kalya said, opening the drawer under the instrument panel and taking out an ordinary looking pair of dark brown framed glasses."

"Can I try them?" Annie asked.

"I don't know if they will work on human eyes," Kalya said, handing them to her.

Annie put the glasses on and immediately stumbled backwards.

"Whoa! These make me dizzy."

"Sit down and give it a minute," said Kalya, motioning for Annie to take a seat on the floor next to the captain's chair. "Your eyes need a little time to adjust."

....

[7] *Gestalt is a German word for "form." The Gestalt effect refers to the ability of our senses, especially our eyes, to recognize figures and shapes, rather than a formless collection of unconnected lines or curves. Our minds automatically add the information necessary to complete a figure. Fivskew screen glasses enhance this tendency even more, so patterns that would otherwise remain hidden suddenly become recognizable.*

"My eyes still feel weird," Annie said a few moments later, "but the room has stopped spinning. I see patterns and forms everywhere!" She looked around the cabin. "I never noticed that bear over there." She pushed the glasses up onto her forehead. "Wait, it's just a bunch of marks on the wall. I can still see the bear shape without the glasses though." She let the glasses fall back down onto the bridge of her nose and looked through them again. "Everything is so vivid. More 3D than 3D." She reached out to touch the instrument panel's screen, but instead her hand waved through the empty air. Puzzled, she pushed the glasses up again so she could peek out from underneath them. The screen was about six inches farther away than she thought.

"These are cool," she exclaimed, looking through the glasses again. "What's that half circle of brown Vs on the map?"

"Half circle?" Kalya asked. "I can see the 'Vs', but not the half circle."

"Don't you see it? It's right over there, in the Forest of Gruwin. Take a look," Annie said, handing Kalya the glasses.

"Oh, I see it now," said Kalya. "Let me run the analyzer," he continued, typing much faster now with his screen glasses on. A small pop-up screen with the symbol key for the map appeared in its upper left-hand corner. The brown Vs were identified as pikdle trees.

"Ah yes, of course," said Kalya. "Those are pikdle trees. I remember reading about them in Mr. Ness's notes. Apparently they are similar to Earth's giant sequoia trees. They also grow to enormous heights. But pikdle trees are unique; their top leaves glow bright red. Even in the dark."

"Wow! Wait a sec," said Annie, staring at the screen. "There's something I didn't notice before—a little tail at the bottom of the horseshoe-shape. It looks like the pendant on Thila Mae's necklace," said Annie, sketching the necklace on the paper with the hole in its middle.

"Why yes," Kalya said, "it does!"

Chapter 23
Ralph's Return

"Arf! Arf!"

"Ralph?" said Annie, looking up in surprise as Ralph bounded down the circular stairs and into the cabin of The Jenny N. "What are you doing here?"

"Arf! Arf!" replied Ralph. Then, remembering he was in Tilania and could speak, he said, "Clayton figured out what is causing the trouble with The Scrolls! He's on Earth trying to stop it. I came to help you."

"What about the Brown Snake?" Annie asked.

"Let me explain," Ralph began, grabbing the corner of his old rumpled cushion in his teeth and dragging it across the floor to the instrument panel. "When Clayton was with Mortimer, that's the brown snake's name, the Disruptors sent him a fake message. Clayton thought it was Mr. Ness trying urgently to reach him, so he rushed home.

He arrived a week before you both jumped into the stamp. While reliving the week, he figured out Dennis is messing up The Scrolls, causing them to disintegrate."

"Dennis? What does Dennis have to do with it? How does he know about The Scrolls?"

"Dennis doesn't realize he's doing anything. He found some purple seeds and planted them for his science project. It turns out the seeds are from Tilania. They are seeds from dedian trees; The Scrolls are made from their bark. Growing the dedian seeds on Earth is causing The Scrolls to fall apart!"

"How did this 'Dennis' get seeds from Tilania?" Kalya asked.

"He found them in Franco's lab. Franco is Dennis's uncle!" Ralph exclaimed.

"He is?" Annie's eyes opened wide.

"Yes! Clayton figured it out."

"But how did Franco bring seeds back from Tilania? He never returned home."

"He had visited Tilania once before. That's when the Disruptors secretly slipped them into his pocket. They wanted Franco to find the seeds and plant them on Earth—but it was Dennis who planted them instead. Clayton stayed behind to retrieve the seeds and plants and bring them back. That will stop any further damage to The Scrolls. But the Disruptors stole a fragment of The Scrolls. We have to find it."

"We know where to look!" Kalya and Annie said in unison. "The Forest of Gruwin."

"On Tondore Island?" Ralph asked.

"That's right. We are headed there now, to the grove of pikdle trees. Thila Mae, from the…What's going on? Why did the engines stop?"

"Because we're here," said Kalya, pointing to a transparent section of the The Jenny N's translucent walls. "That, is Tondore Island."

Chapter 24
Tondore Island

"Ralph…it's happening again!" Annie said, pointing to the flattened fur on Ralph's back.

Ralph circled round and round, craning his head over his shoulder in a vain attempt to get a look.

"It is a horseshoe-shape," Kalya explained.

"I wish I could see my 'readings'—that's what Mr. Ness always calls them."

"You mean like Aunt Jenny's tea leaf readings?" asked Annie.

"Yeah. I never know when one is going to appear. This horseshoe, it must mean something."

"It does," Annie exclaimed. "Take a look at this." She gestured to the map with one hand and held up her drawing with the other. "The grove of pikdle trees and

Thila Mae's necklace are both in the shape of a horseshoe. And now it's in your fur."

"Are those brown things pikdle trees?" Ralph asked, studying the map.

"Yes. The Disruptors tried to distract us by leaving their marks all over Tondore Island, but we discovered the horseshoe-shaped grove. That's where we'll find them."

"Annie, hand me your MRVD," said Kalya. "I'll download everything for your journey."

"My journey? Aren't you coming?"

"No, you go on with Ralph. I'll go back to Nessen and wait for Clayton."

"There it is again," Annie said, watching the fur on Ralph's back flatten into the horseshoe-shape once more.

Ralph craned his neck once again trying to see it. "Who is Thila Mae?" he asked, shaking out his fur.

"Thila Mae is the air Travel Current mechanic," Annie answered, yanking open the small circular door cut in the floor next to the instrument panel. "She told Kalya and me to go the Forest of Gruwin," she continued, climbing down the ladder into the hold of the ship, Ralph following close behind. She untied the spare rowboat and pulled it down the ramp into the water. When she reached the end of the docking bay, she secured the boat with the rope and climbed aboard while Ralph jumped in.

"What's all this stuff growing in the water?" she asked, untying the rowboat and turning it towards the shore. "It feels like I'm rowing through molasses."

"That's the problem with Solano Bay," Ralph answered. "It's a marsh."

Every stroke was a struggle for Annie. Clumps of plants and reeds clung to the oars, and the murky water made it hard to determine the best way through. As the rowboat crept towards the shore, the plants grew taller and thicker, crowding in on either side, scratching Annie's arms and face.

Annie freed an oar from its lock and tested the depth of the water. "It's pretty shallow here," she said, pulling the oars into the boat. "It'll be quicker to drop anchor and wade the rest of way."

Nodding in agreement, Ralph lifted the anchor with his two front paws and tossed it overboard. It slowly sank through the tangle of plants.

Annie rolled up her pant legs and took off her shoes and socks. She stuffed her socks inside her shoes, tied the laces together and slung them over her shoulder. After taking a long look at the thick blanket of grasses, rushes, and reeds stretching out in front of her, she pushed her bangs out of her eyes, climbed out and began trudging to shore.

Ralph slipped out of the boat, careful not to splash Annie. "It's not so bad," he said.

"Easy for you to say," Annie replied. "You're swimming, you don't have to touch the icky bottom."

Her feet sank down into the soft, slimy muck. It oozed between her toes and made a sucking sound each time she lifted a foot free. When she reached the shore, she climbed up onto the rocks. "Yuck," she said in disgust, looking down at her mucky feet.

"There's a stream over here," Ralph called out, trying not to laugh at Annie's funny-looking scrunched-up face. "Come on over. You can rinse off your feet."

Annie climbed over the rocks and stepped into the crystal-clear water. She bent down and scrubbed her feet while Ralph swam nearby, vigorously shaking the mud and silt out of his fur. When Annie was satisfied that her feet were sufficiently clean, she sat down and dried them with one of her socks. Then, she untied her laces and put on the remaining sock and her shoes.

"That must be the path up there," she said, checking the map on her MRVD. Then, with her MRVD in one back pocket of her jeans and her single wet sock sticking out of the other, she started over the rocks, Ralph trotting along behind her.

Chapter 25

B. B. Gene

The path led Annie and Ralph through a narrow valley surrounded on both sides by a series of rolling hills. Then it opened onto a meadow of grass and sedge, occasionally passing thickets of pale-barked trees whose silver coin-shaped leaves rustled in the wind.

Annie stopped to tie her shoe when a squat, white, wooly-haired creature tottered onto the path and plopped down in front of her and Ralph. It had large droopy eyes, long floppy ears, and wore a red felted pack on its back.

"It is a good thing…you came today…Annie," the creature began in a low, quivering voice. "Tomorrow… would have been…too late."

"You know me?" Annie asked.

"Of course…I do. Thila Mae…has told me…all about you. I have been…waiting for you…to come. And who," he said, tilting his head towards Ralph, "are you?"

"Ralph. Who are you?"

"I am…B.B. Gene. Welcome to…Tondore Island. As you well know, the Disruptors…have been busy here."

"We mapped the location of all their marks," said Annie. "But we couldn't find any disruptions."

"That is because…these disruptions…are different from…all others. They are…the work of…The Three."

"The Three?" Annie asked.

"That is the name…we have…given them. They are… three who broke away…from the rest. The Three…are corrupt…and greedy. They want…to take over!"

"Take over what?" Ralph asked.

"Tilania…and the Underworld. They seek…to control us all."

"Does this have something to do with The Scrolls?" Ralph asked.

"There is…much to tell," said B.B. "But you must…be patient. I am afraid…the longer I talk, the slower…I speak. Please…sit down," he continued, nodding towards a small clearing nearby. "The moss…is soft." His legs creaked as he rose slowly, tottered to the clearing, and sank down, tucking his front hoofs beneath him gingerly.

Once Annie and Ralph were seated, B.B. Gene continued. "I will begin with the Legend…of the Elements."

"Mr. Ness told me that the Legend of the Elements has been mostly forgotten," said Ralph.

"I am afraid, this is true. Much of it…is no longer known. But…its core message…is still widely remembered…by all living things in Tilania…and the in Underworld. It continues…to be passed down…from generation…to generation."

B.B. Gene paused, rested for a moment, then went on. "From the beginning…Tilania… and the Underworld… have celebrated…Four Elements: Earth, Air, Water…and Fire…."

"Hey, that's a rock band," Annie interrupted. "No, wait, that's not right, its 'Earth, Wind and Fire,' Oh….I'm sorry B. B. Gene," she continued, embarrassed by her sudden outburst. "Please go on."

"In addition…to these Four Elements…there is also…a Fifth. One we…do not celebrate, Chaos."

"What do you mean by Chaos?" Ralph asked.

"Chaos…is when…the natural order of the world… is disrupted. Everything…is confused…and thrown out of balance. Nothing…is the way…it is supposed to be."

"But that can happen anytime, can't it?" asked Annie. "Things aren't always the way I expect." At that moment, the stick she was using to dig a pebble out of the bottom of her shoe snapped in two with a loud thwack.

"Like this," she laughed, holding up the two broken pieces, one in each hand.

"That…is true. Sometimes…unexpected things…do happen. But Chaos…is different. Should it exist…Tilania… and the Underworld…would be thrown…into a total state…of confusion and disarray. The laws of nature… would no longer…exist. The seasons…might become…

unpredictable—snow storms in summer…and heat waves in winter. The rain…instead of pouring down, could shoot up…into the sky. The force of gravity…could alter—so strong…no one would be able…to lift their legs…to walk, or so weak…they might float…into the sky."

B.B. Gene gave a long, loud sigh and continued, "No living being…would want such Chaos."

"What does this have to do with The Three?" asked Annie.

"The Legend…forbids carrying…the Five Elements— Earth, Air, Water, Fire, and…Chaos—over The Great Falls," said B.B. Gene, clearing his throat with a deep *baaaaaaaaa*. "This…is exactly…what The Three…are determined…to do."

"I don't get it, why would that be so bad?"

"If anyone…or anything…succeeded in doing this, they would rule…our worlds. No one…should ever be granted…such power."

"How can you 'capture' all Five Elements?" asked Annie.

"That…is a fine question. You…must understand, according to the legend, it is…only a bit of each element… that is needed.

"If The Three…were to touch…all Five Elements— Earth, Air, Water, Fire…and Chaos—and go over…The Great Falls of Gruwin, their power…would immediately flourish…and grow. Power…of this sort…is like a weed… that takes over everything. Their…control of others… would invade our worlds…and destroy our way of life."

"Wait," Ralph shouted. "Clayton told me that The Scrolls are disintegrating. The Disruptors stole a piece. That disintegrating piece could be the 'bit' of Chaos they need!

"The Three must have caused the disintegration of The Scrolls, and then stolen a fragment. They must be getting ready to go over The Great Falls with all Five Elements."

"I'm afraid so," said B.B. Gene. "And…Thila Mae is convinced…The Three are going to try…to do it this very evening, just…as the sun…begins to set."

"We need to get to The Great Falls!" said Annie. "Can you take us there B.B. Gene?"

"I wish I could…but I am…much too old…to make the trip. I walk…even slower…than I talk. If I were to go, we would never…get there…in time to stop The Three."

"Can you show us the fastest way to go?" Annie asked, pointing to the map of the Forest of Gruwin on her MRVD.

"My eyes…are too weak. But, I can describe…where it is. First, find the grove…of pikdle trees."

"We know where that is," said Annie, confidently. "The grove is in the shape of Thila Mae's necklace, a horseshoe with a little line sticking out at the bottom like on the letter Q."

"Yes,…the grove is special…to Thila Mae. That bit…at the bottom of the horseshoe…is where The Wide River… flows into…The Great Falls. Stop The Three…there."

Their conversation was interrupted by a faint faraway clinking sound. "Do you hear that noise?" asked Ralph. "It sounds like wind chimes."

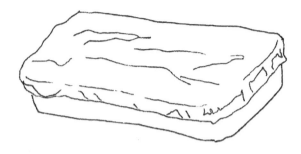

Chapter 26
The Plan

"Thila Mae?" Annie called out, scanning the horizon. "Is that you up there?"

"Got this darn kink in my left landing gear," came a reply from atop a nearby tree. "Down in two shakes. Need to stretch out a bit."

With that, Thila Mae rose high into the air, flew three perfect figure eights, and descended, almost knocking down B.B. Gene as she landed heavily, her left wing partially extended.

"Would you believe. Landing gear's stuck again. Coulda bonked you clear over B.B. Good thing you're steady on your feet. Thing is, lost my Thimbit," she continued, staring at the empty loop on the front of her tool belt. "Can't fix the gear without it. Gotta be around here somewhere. Anyone seen it?"

Not pausing to take a breath or to let anyone answer, Thila Mae extended a right wing to Ralph and kept on chattering. "Thilamaeteknision. Glad to meet you. Ralph's your name, isn't it? Giving them the lowdown on The Three, B.B.?

"Woke up this morning and it hit me. Plain as the beak on my face. Today's the day the're going to do it. Got it all figured out, vibes fit—five bits. Earth-Air-Fire-Water-Chaos. Take those five bits over The Great Falls and whammo! It's over. Got to stop them before the sun sets. Good thing you've got a plan."

"Plan?" asked Annie. "We're heading to the grove, if that's what you mean."

"The grove's the ticket, alright. I found…what the? Hold it right there a sec, folks. Got to do what you got to do when you got to do it," Thila Mae said, stretching out her left wing. Out plopped a shiny metal object that looked like an old fashioned eggbeater, but without the handle. "Well, I never. How'd my Thimbit end up in my landing gear? Ah, that sure feels a whole lot better. Now where was I?"

"You were saying…the grove's the ticket." B.B. Gene reminded her, his voice slow and shaky.

"Right you are. The grove. Flew there this morning," Thila Mae chuckled. "Saw what The Three are up to. But not to worry, no big deal if they saw me. Nothing suspicious about me flying 'round the grove. Do it all the time. My favorite spot in all of Gruwin. Or anywhere else, come to think of it." Thila Mae stopped talking long enough to lift up her horseshoe-shaped pendant and gaze at it fondly. "Got a soft spot for those giant pikdle trees. Every last one of them."

"Thila Mae," Annie interrupted. "What was it you saw?"

119

"Saw a canoe in the bushes. No can do without a canoe! If you catch my drift. Trap them right there. Ever heard the music of those pikdle trees? All you need is one. And a good stiff breeze. Hear that music once and I'll guarantee you'll never forget it. Sweet as the taste of honey. Speaking of which. Baked you your favorite casserole B.B. Got it right here in my toolbox." Thila Mae flipped open her tool box lid and took out a large aluminum covered dish and placed it in the red felted pack on B. B. Gene's back. "Wrapped it up nice and tight. Still plenty hot. Succotash. With lots of sharp cheddar cheese. Crispy bacon too. Just the way you like it.

"I'd best be going," said Thila Mae, taking to the air, tipping her left wing and circling twice. "Mind the bugs," she shouted down. "Darn bites itch so much, once you start scratching, you can't stop." Then she flew out of sight.

"'No can do without a canoe'?" Annie asked.

"The Three…need a way…to go over The Great Falls," B.B. Gene answered, "They must be using…a canoe."

"And if we find the canoe we will know where they are," Annie explained to Ralph and B.B. Gene.

"Oh, what I would not give…to be young and spry… once again. Good luck," said B.B. Gene.

"So long," said Ralph.

"Nice to have met you," Annie added, as B.B. Gene raised himself slowly, his backpack almost toppling off from the effort.

"Goodbye," said B.B. Gene, in the strongest voice he could muster.

Chapter 27
A Short Cut

Annie and Ralph continued on the path to the Forest of Gruwin, climbing a series of switchbacks that led up a steep hillside. When they reached the crest of the hill, they saw the forest spread out below, and in the distance the grove of pikdle trees, their towering tops glowing bright red, just as Kalya had described. As the path began its descent, they entered the forest. Slivers of sunshine peeked through the tall pine trees, scattering patterns of light onto the path. The murmur of rushing water from the nearby stream and occasional bird song were the only sounds Annie and Ralph heard.

After almost an hour of brisk walking, they came to a large boulder, which completely blocked the path. They circled around it, Annie to the left, Ralph to the right.

"Where's the path?" Annie asked. "I can't find it, can you?"

"No. Maybe it starts up again on the other side of this

clump of bushes. Follow me," Ralph said, disappearing inside them.

"Ouch!" Annie said. "Something just bit me."

"It's the bushes. They're prickly. Watch out for them," Ralph called out.

"It's not the bushes. It's those bugs Thila Mae warned us about." Annie shouted, slapping at her arms. "Ouch! They keep biting me. I can't see them, but I can hear them buzzing all around my head. They're like no-see ums."

"Don't scratch, whatever you do."

"But the itching is driving me crazy."

"Don't do it. It will just make it worse," Ralph warned. "We'll put some medicine on it."

"You have medicine?"

"Yes. Elephant tulips. They'll stop the itching. That's what Mr. Ness always used when he got bitten. He taught me how to make a poultice. We'll use mud from the stream."

"I'm so itchy, I'll try anything," said Annie, stepping out the bushes, furiously scratching at the tiny red welts covering both her arms.

Ralph sat on his hind legs, reached up with his front paws, and unzipped the small pocket on the front of the leather collar he always wore. A little bundle of dried orange flowers tied with a string tumbled out.

"These are dried elephant tulip flowers from the banks of Five-Sided Lake," he said, pulling at the string to open the bundle. "Hold these while I get some mud."

He grasped a long stick between his teeth, trotted to the nearby stream, and began digging in the muddy bank. Returning to Annie, he dropped the mud-covered stick on the ground beside her.

"Put a small piece of dried flower on each bite and then press some mud on top of it. That will hold it in place. The itching will go away once the mud dries. You'll see."

Annie put a piece of dried elephant tulip flower and a blob of mud on each bite. When the mud dried, the itching disappeared, just as Ralph had promised.

"I wish we had medicine for mosquito bites that worked this fast," Annie said, as she and Ralph started down the path again. "I never noticed that pocket on your collar before. What else is in there?"

"Not much. It's pretty small. It just has the dried elephant tulips and some stuff for Mr. Ness's handheld fireballs."

"Handheld fireballs are so cool. I never knew Mr. Ness made them."

"He does, but not at home. Mrs. Ness doesn't like it."

"I researched them for my science project, but I never got to make one. Ms. Warren said doing a project with fire was against the school's safety policy. I guess that makes sense," Annie shrugged. "Anyway, I know how to make them too. It's easy. You make a small ball out of material that only burns at a high temperature, and you use fuel that can burn at a low temperature. That way, the fire will burn the fuel, but it won't burn the ball—so, you can hold the ball in your hand while the fuel is burning.

"You have to remember not touch the flame though,

because that part is really hot. It could burn you. The science book I read said the best way to hold a fireball is in the palm of your hand, so only the bottom part touches your skin. The ball gets about as hot as a cookie that has just come out of the oven.[8]

The path narrowed and became rocky. The stream changed its course, and flowed across the path to the other side. Annie hopped from rock to rock, carefully fording across, and Ralph ran to join her.

"Wait, I've got it," Annie cried out. "A handheld fireball. That's a way The Three could hold 'a bit of fire.'"

"Wouldn't it be simpler for them to just use a torch?" Ralph asked.

"But they have to be touching the fire, remember?"

"Wouldn't the fireball go out if it's windy?"

"Not necessarily. Once it's burning, it's hard to put it out. And, once…"Annie stopped talking. Just ahead, to the right of the path, was a giant red door with a shiny brass door knob in its center. The door wasn't leading anywhere, or locking anything in or out. It simply stood in the middle of the forest, like a sculpture.

"What is a door doing here?" Annie asked.

"Better here than there," Thila Mae called out from atop a nearby pine tree. "That's what I always say. Never can tell when a door might come in handy."

"Hello," Annie and Ralph shouted up in unison, craning their necks to catch a glimpse of Thila Mae as she tipped

....

[8] *Kids, do not try this at home unless supervised by an adult.*

124

her green and yellow plaid cap to them.

"Greetings. Nothing like a brisk walk through the forest. Of course, prefer flying myself. Beautiful day isn't it? Enough to warm your cockles. Never seen one, mind you. A cockle I mean. Kind of like a clam, I hear. Heart-shaped. Tasty too. A bit salty though."

"Who put this here?" Ralph asked, gesturing to the door.

"Door came on its own, if that's what you mean. Whew," Thila Mae let out a shrill whistle. "Wow, take a look at that paint job."

"You mean the door's?" Annie asked.

"Sure looks good. Don't you think? Ruby red. Nice a color as I've ever seen. And that's a fact. Door's got to feel good about itself after all! Needs to look the part. Keep its hinges shiny and its brass polished. Got an important job to do."

"What job?" asked Annie. "Why is it here?"

"For going out and coming in. Got to get where you got to get, when you got to get there, don't you? Now, what's that rhyme? Had it right here on the tip of my tongue. Got it," Thila Mae exclaimed.

Red door, green floor

Nothing but gravy in the navy

Lots of…lots of…

"*Hmmm*…how's the rest of it go? Where'd I put my rhyming book? Could have sworn. Nope. Not in my toolbox. Must have left it…need a rhyme to get that door open. I'll get down there right quick."

Thila Mae swooped down and landed with a loud thud, just inches from the big red door. She took a giant step back with her left leg, bent down on her right knee, swept her green and yellow plaid cap off her head, and bowed low…

We've travelled near

And journeyed far

Red door in the forest

Now come ajar

"Remembered that one clear through! Ought to do the trick. Go ahead Annie. Give it a whirl. Open her up."

Annie stepped up to the giant red door. Standing on her tiptoes, she reached up and tried the doorknob. It didn't budge.

"It's locked," she said.

"Phooey! Best to leave it alone. Just let it be. Door's got to be asleep for the short cut to work. Wake it up, you're asking for trouble. Going to forget all about it. The shortcut I mean. Wipe the slate clean. Like it never was."

Annie and Ralph exchanged puzzled looks.

"Shortcut?" asked Ralph.

A short cut is never

In front of your eyes

The right way, the wrong way

It's no surprise

"No idea where that one came from. Just popped right into my head," said Thila Mae. "Never heard it before. Not in my rhyming book."

126

There was a short click, followed by a loud creak.

S-S-S-W-W-W-O-O-O-S-S-S-H-H-H!! Thila Mae dropped her hat in surprise as the giant, red door swung open.

"I'll be! Looks like we're in luck. Must have been the right rhyme," said Thila Mae, peering through the door and pointing to the scene in front of her with the tip of her left wing. "Take a look. See for yourself. One step through the door and just like that, we're smack-dab in the middle of the grove of pikdle trees. Pretty as a picture. Don't you think?"

Framed by the open door, a narrow path led straight ahead into the center of the horseshoe-shaped grove of towering red-tipped pikdle trees, their tops soaring high into the sky. Green ferns and moss-covered rocks blanketed the forest floor, and here and there purple and orange flowers added splashes of color.

"*Shhh!* Take a listen," said Thila Mae. "Hear the wind rustling through the leaves? Love that sound, don't you? Makes me want to sing. You know that one about rowing down the stream? Never been in a rowboat myself. Come to think of it. But paddled a canoe once. Hard thing to steer. Lots bigger then the one they've got hidden. The Three I mean. Got to get to that canoe before they do.

"Time to get a move on. Never can tell, this door might change its mind. Step right up, on, over and through. Lickety-split. Full speed ahead. I'll go first. Show you where they hid it," said Thila Mae, tucking her wings close to her body, bending down her head, and waddling through the open door, her cap barely clearing the top of the doorframe.

Chapter 28

Tail of the Horseshoe

Annie and Ralph followed Thila Mae through the doorway and onto the path that led into the horseshoe-shaped grove of pikdle trees, closing the big, red door behind them.

"Never been on this shortcut myself," Thila Mae shouted over her shoulder, waddling along in front of Annie and Ralph. "Can't recollect the last time I walked anywhere. But there's a first time for everything. That's what I always say. Take norps for instance. You ever try eating one? There's a taste that takes some getting used to. Got a big crop growing on the Isle of Hearts. Not far from the settlement. Secret is to mix them with lots of sliced wetzels. Do that and you got yourself a great meal. You ought to try it. Just had some yesterday. Sure is getting dark on this path, isn't it. Ouch. Almost tripped on a rock.

Good thing I got my boots on. Darn these tree roots. Sticking out everywhere. Can't see a thing."

Annie, Ralph, and Thila Mae had reached the bottom of the horseshoe, where the towering pikdle trees grew tightly together, blocking out the sun and leaving the path in darkness. Annie slowed her pace, reached out her arms, and began groping her way along the path. "Oh, the Nocto-Vision," she muttered to herself, reaching into her pocket and pressing the orange button on her MRVD. Within seconds her eyes could see in the dark.

"Kalya got the Nocto-Vision working?" Ralph asked, trotting beside her. His dog eyes had naturally adapted to the darkness as it fell.

"Wait up! You are both faster than fast," Thila Mae called out, falling farther and farther behind. "Fixed Kalya's screen glasses but never picked up the Nocto…Nocto…what's it called again?" Thila Mae asked.

"Nocto-Vision," Anne answered, stopping to let Thila Mae catch up.

"Seeing in the dark. That's the trick. But, if you can't see, you can always feel," Thila Mae said, waddling closer. She lifted her left wing tip and began pulling gently on a loose thread at the bottom of her polka-dot vest.

"I'll hold it here and you hold it there," she instructed, snapping off the thread and handing one end to Annie.

"Oh, okay, I get it. But won't it break if I tug it? It looks pretty thin."

"Just hold it loose. Never met a touch I couldn't feel. Keep a good pace," Thila Mae said, holding her end of the string in her wing.

No way I can see

'Cuz I don't have N-V!

But long as I feel

I still got a deal

Thila Mae chuckled to herself.

They continued down the narrow path in single file. Ralph led the way, then Annie, holding the thread lightly in her right hand, and finally Thila Mae, waddling fast enough to keep the thin thread hanging lax between herself and Annie.

After some time, the dark path through the band of pikdle trees ended, and Ralph, Annie and Thila Mae emerged into the daylight again. Ahead they saw the sparkling blue waters of The Wide River and heard its rushing roar.

"There's the tail of the horseshoe!" said Annie, pointing to the thin line of pikdle trees veering off to the left of the path.

"Time to take to the air. Great view on top!" said Thila Mae, half hopping, half flying from branch to branch, steadily working her way higher and higher, until she reached the top of the pikdle trees and the open sky.

"Humpus pumpus on the blow horn," she called down, as she opened her wings and flew off across The Wide River and descended onto its far bank.

As soon as she landed, she began flapping her wings, hopping up and down and shouting to Annie and Ralph. But the roaring waters of The Great Falls wiped away the sound of her words. Whatever it was she was trying to tell them must have been important, because she kept right on shouting.

Then she stopped shouting, and instead of flying back, stepped into the rushing waters of The Wide River. She swam straight across, unimpeded by the force of the swift current.

"Stand back!" Thila Mae yelled, as she waddled ashore, forgetting she was now close enough to be heard. She anchored her long, spindly legs, put her head down, and furiously flapped her wings, water shooting out in all directions.

"That ought to do it," she said with a satisfied grin, drawing her wings close to her body. "Oops. Almost forgot my rudder," she continued, briskly wagging her tail feathers from side to side. "Steers me across, straight as an arrow, every time. No way I would cross any closer to the falls, mind you. Not with that current. Adventure's what I'm after, not danger."

Thila Mae took off her green and yellow plaid cap, her brown and white polka-dot vest, and her leather tool belt, and hung them on nearby branches to dry. "Need a hand with these boots. Laces get wet and they're a pain to undo."

Annie bent down and untied Thila Mae's wet laces.

"Start with this one," said Thila Mae, wrapping her wings around the nearest pikdle tree and lifting her left boot high in the air. "Give it a hard yank."

Annie pulled hard on each boot, struggling not to lose her balance and fall over when each of Thila Mae's feet came free.

"Can barely feel my toes. Always forget how cold that water is. Refreshing though. Got to get these wet socks off. Trick is to roll them all the way down. Piece of cake after that. There you go," Thila Mae said, peeling off one sock and then the other. "Ah, sure feels good to wiggle my toes," she went on, waddling barefoot into the bushes to the left of the path.

"Can't find where it's at," her muffled voice called out. "The canoe I mean. Darned if it hasn't gone missing. Could have sworn it was hidden right here," Thila Mae continued, poking her head out over the top of the bushes. "Wait a sec. Did I mix up my left and my right again? Always doing that. Can't remember that darn trick. The one that figures out what's left and what's right. Wouldn't happen to know it, would you? Tried tying a green string on my bootlaces once. Problem was forgot if I tied it on my left or my right. Better take a look over there."

Thila Mae waddled to the bushes on the other side of the path. "Bingo! Wouldn't you know. Here all along."

Chapter 29
Setting the Trap

The dark-green wooden canoe was surprisingly tiny, no bigger than a child's wagon. It was resting upside-down on a pair of small sawhorses on the grass next to the bank of The Wide River.

"*Psst! Psst!*" Ralph whispered, peeking his head out from behind a nearby pikdle tree.

"No need to hide. Come take a look," said Thila Mae.

"What about The Three?" Ralph whispered. "Won't they see us?"

"Never can tell if they're here or if they're there. That's the truth. But this time of day, only one place The Three can be. Or any Disruptors, for that matter. Digging up breg bulbs. Now where did I put my cap?" Thila Mae asked, patting the top of her head with one wing. "Wait a minute, oh yeah, over there," she said, spying her clothes hanging on branches nearby. She waddled over to retrieve them. "Now where was I? Ah, breg bulbs. Don't care much for them myself. Only thing Disruptors ever want to eat. Afternoon's the time to do it. Dig them up I mean. Heat of the day. That's when they rise to the top. Grow in the southern part of Tondore Island. The Three will be gone 'til dusk."

"Their canoe is so small," Annie exclaimed, taking out one of its wooden paddles. "Look how tiny this is!"

"Perfect when you're the size of a hedgehog."

"How do you know how big they are?" asked Ralph. "No one has ever seen them."

"Don't know how I know. Just know that I know."

"How big is a hedgehog?" Ralph asked.

"I remember reading about them. They're about the size of a baseball," said Annie.

"Baseball. Now there's a game I'd like to see. Always chewing gum, baseball players I mean. Ever try that sticky stuff?" Thila Mae asked.

The mention of the word sticky, gave Annie an idea. "Can you get sap from pikdle trees, Thila Mae?" she asked.

"Sap? Sure thing. Tapped some myself last time I was here. A bit tricky at first. But once you get the hang of it, easy as pie. Filled a whole bucket. Got it stashed in my pantry," Thila Mae continued, opening her toolkit. "Take these with me wherever I go," she said, handing Annie a shiny metal drill, matching spigot, and small pail. "Be prepared. That's my motto. Same as the Boy Scouts. Never met one mind you." Thila Mae stopped chattering, shielded her eyes with her left wing, and gazed up at the sun. "Three o'clock already. No wonder I'm tired. Don't mind if I take a snooze, do you?" she asked, as she lay down in front of the nearest pikdle tree, pulled her long, spindly legs up under her wings, tipped her green and yellow plaid cap over her eyes, and fell fast asleep.

"Hold these," Annie said, handing Ralph the shiny spigot and the small pail.

"What are you doing?"

"I'm going to collect some sap for the trap."

"Oh, I get it."

"Which tree should we tap?"

"The one with the biggest trunk, I guess. How about that one over there?"

Annie took off her shoe and, using its heel as a hammer, banged the sharp end of the drill into the pikdle tree. When she was satisfied the drill was secure, she screwed it into the tree until most of it disappeared inside the trunk.

"I think that's deep enough," said Annie. "Hand me the spigot."

While Ralph positioned the pail underneath, Annie shoved the spigot into place and turned it on. A thick band of amber-colored sap began to flow, twisting round and round as it fell into the pail.

When the pail was half-full Annie turned off the spigot. "That's plenty. Now what we need is a brush."

"Brush?" asked Thila Mae, springing wide awake and bending down to put on her boots. "Look no further! Got more tail feathers than I know what to do with. Used one myself just the other day. Painted my brother Max's old shed. Purple. That's his favorite color. Looks pretty good."

Chapter 30

Hovering

The moment Clayton jumped, he knew something was different. Mr. Ness's banjo music sounded eerie and slowed down, the spaces between each note drawn out. The soles of his feet tickled as if someone was stroking them with a feather.

He floated towards the stamp. When his toes finally touched its surface, instead of falling into the rowboat, he hovered above it. Bright ribbons of purple, green and yellow lights flashed and shimmered all around him.

As the banjo music grew fainter, the lights grew brighter. They darted and danced, faster and faster, in a mesmerizing display of color against the blue, cloudless sky.

Gradually losing altitude, Clayton finally landed in the rowboat. Flash! The sky lit up in a dazzling burst of light. Then the ribbons disappeared, leaving behind faint wisps of color. They looked like trails left in the wake of a jet plane, or the smoky residue of a fireworks display.

The Jenny N was anchored nearby. Clayton placed the box with the two dedian plants in the bottom of the boat and clapped his hands twice. The Jenny N's entry system activated. The translucent walkway unfurled and came to rest next to the rowboat. Clayton climbed out onto the walkway and bent down to retrieve the dedian plants.

"Well done! I see you have the plants," Kalya shouted down from the open hatch door.

"That was weird," Clayton said, as he climbed up the rope ladder clutching a plant in his right arm. He handed it to Kalya and then went to retrieve the other.

Once inside, he plopped down on the floor and let out a loud yawn.

"I'm so tired," he yawned again. "Where's Annie?" he asked, looking around the ship.

"Annie is with Ralph. You're tired because you hovered for over two hours! I've been watching you," Kalya explained. "I've read about the hovering effect. It's supposed to be very tiring because of the stimulation. Did you notice anything unusual?"

"Yes! There were these bright colored lights all over the sky—like the northern lights."

"You mean the Aurora Borealis?"

"Yeah, like them. They were awesome! I could see them really well even though it was daylight. They were there the whole time I hovered—but it only felt like a few minutes. Did you see them?"

"No. You saw them because you were in a hovering state."

Clayton yawned loudly again and sank down on Ralph's cushion.

"Where are the seeds? Did you bring them?"

"I've got them right here," Clayton answered, patting his pocket. Then rubbing his eyes and yawning again, he lay his head down on the cushion.

"Then we are ready to go to Tondore Island," Kalya said. He sat down in the captain's chair, engaged the thrusters and began the journey.

"Tondore…?" Clayton started to ask as he drifted off to sleep.

Chapter 31
Solano Bay

"Clayton! Clayton! Wake up," Kalya said, poking him in the shoulder with his right front tentacle.

"Mmmm, what did you say?" Clayton mumbled, opening his eyes and looking at Kalya with a dazed expression. For a moment he had forgotten where he was.

"We're almost at Tondore Island. We'll meet Annie and Ralph at the grove of pikdle trees." Kalya explained, pointing to the collection of brown V's on the map in the Forest of Gruwin.

"Why there?" asked Clayton, smoothing out his tousled hair and slowly getting to his feet.

"Because that is where we think the Disruptors are."

"That's the same horseshoe-shape I saw in the sky," Clayton exclaimed, examining the map.

"The lights were in a shape?"

"Yeah, after they stopped shimmering they were. They left a trail in the sky and it looked just like that—a horseshoe with a little tail at the bottom."

"Annie said Thila Mae wore a pendant in that shape, too."

"Who is Thila Mae?"

"She is the air Travel Current mechanic," Kalya began, "Annie met her when the Travel Current broke. She sent an anagram message for me, 'twig in virus.' Annie unscrambled it; it means, visit Gruwin. That is how we knew where to look for the Disruptors. Did Mortimer mention the Forest of Gruwin?"

"Never. How come you always call him 'the brown snake' if you know his name is Mortimer?" Clayton asked.

"The brown snake clans are very secretive as you must now well understand. Do they know about the dedian plants?"

"No—they didn't know Dennis was growing them," Clayton said.

"Now that the dedian seeds are back in their natural habitat, we should give them to the birds to eat. Here, use this," Kalya instructed, handing Clayton a tray that looked like a small baking sheet, except for one concave edge. "Go up the ladder and attach this feeder outside the hatch door."

"Alright," Clayton said, taking the tray and climbing the circular stairs. He opened the hatch and looked down at the curved outer wall of the ship. "Where do I put it?" he shouted down to Kalya.

"Anywhere. Just press the concave edge of the tray to the curved wall of ship. It will bond to it."

Clayton matched the tray's curved edge to the outside of the ship. It instantly adhered and formed a shelf. He sprinkled the seeds on the tray and headed down the stairs. "Cool," he exclaimed. "How does that work?"

"The properties of the ship's walls allow bonding with certain types of metal," Kalya explained, picking up a watering can next to the sink. He filled it and watered both dedian plants.

"I think it's too late for that one," said Clayton, pointing to the shriveled up plant. "It looks dead to me."

"I'm taking it to the hospital," said Kalya, placing it with a few other struggling potted plants gathered in the corner next the sink. "Five drops ought to do it," he continued, unscrewing the top of a small vial filled with orange liquid.

"What's that?" asked Clayton.

"Mr. Ness calls it 'Orangeade.' It is a protein liquid that will rejuvenate the plant if there is any life left in it."

"There sure doesn't seem to be any life left in those other ones," Clayton said, looking skeptically at the dying dedian plant's sad companions.

"Yes, that is true," Kalya agreed. "But dedian plants are hardy." When he was finished watering the plants he opened a drawer underneath the instrument panel and took out a bin filled with brown booties.

"What are these?" Clayton asked, picking through the pile. The booties were made of a thick rubber-like material.

"My hikers," Kalya answered.

"Hikers?" Clayton asked, not quite stifling a laugh. "You mean like hiking boots?"

"Yes, hikers," Kalya answered sharply, beginning to put them on. "Unless you plan on carrying me all the way to the grove, I need something that will protect my tentacles." He clasped the last hiker clumsily between his already shoed front two tentacles and shoved it on, his droopy eyes stern.

"Okay. Sorry. I didn't mean to get under your skin…er, shell," Clayton said, trying his hardest to sound serious. "Do we have a map of where we're going?"

"Ah, I almost forgot to download everything onto your MRVD," Kalya replied.

Clayton realized he was wearing his suit again. He reached into his pocket and found his MRVD.

"Just hold it up to the screen," Kalya said, fumbling to push the correct button on the control with his front left hiker. "There. Got it."

"Your clothes are over there. I retrieved them from the Passageway," Kalya explained, pointing to Clayton's duffel bag.

Clayton changed and put his MRVD into the front pocket of his jeans. "Are we swimming ashore?" he asked, as he yanked open the circular door and started down the ladder.

"No. We'll take the spare rowboat. It is below, in the hold."

"What's all of this yucky stuff?" Clayton asked, pulling at the weeds and mucky vegetation caked all over the boat. He untied it and pulled it down the ramp.

"I didn't have time to clean it after I retrieved it from the marsh," Kalya answered, plodding down the ramp behind Clayton.

"Are you sure you can walk in those things?" Clayton asked, poking a finger into the front of one of Kalya's hikers.

"Please, just start rowing."

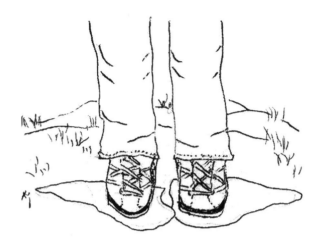

Chapter 32

Getting to the Grove

Clayton and Kalya rowed towards Tondore Island. When the thick vegetation of the marsh became too dense to go on, they anchored the boat and climbed overboard to wade ashore.

"*Blagh!*" Clayton groaned, scrambling out of the water and looking down at his mud caked shoes and jeans. "Gross," he said, wiping off a glop with his finger. "Look at you," he laughed, glancing over at Kalya.

Kalya had crawled up onto the rocks, a disgusted look on his face. His shell was completely covered with muck; he looked like a large muddy blob wearing boots.

"I should have swam instead of walking on the bottom," Kalya said. "I wanted to break in my hikers."

"Do you hear that? It's running water," Clayton said, as he climbed over the rocks. As soon as he spied the stream, he stepped into its clean, clear water, shoes and all. Kalya scurried over to join him. When he emerged, his shell and hikers were free of debris.

"Not one drop got inside!" he said proudly, waving a hiker in the air as they headed down the path. "The waterproofing worked."

"I wish I could say the same," said Clayton, sloshing along beside him.

....

They followed the path through the narrow valley and into the sedge and grass-filled meadow. After winding through the series of switchbacks to the crest of the hill, they descended into the Forest of Gruwin, just as Annie and Ralph had done. But when they reached the large boulder which blocked the path, Kalya warned, "Go around. Don't go through those prickly bushes. They are filled with bugs."

"Here's the path," Clayton shouted from the far side of the bushes. He watched as Kalya trudged up after him, each step awkward and deliberate.

"Are your tentacles okay?" he asked, chuckling.

"Never been better," Kalya replied emphatically, picking up his pace and charging ahead.

Clayton soon forgot all about teasing Kalya; they had reached the big red door. "What's that?" he asked, his mouth agape.

"Ah, it's true. A Door of Tondore," Kalya exclaimed.

"In my studies I learned about them. They are shortcuts around the Island."

"Like the passageways from Tilania and the Isle of Hearts to the Underworld?"

"Sort of...but these aren't slides or steep stairways, and they don't go from one world to another. They are shortcuts on given paths."

"You mean these doors can take you all over Tilania?"

"No, just Tondore Island. No one knows who put them here. There are supposed to be three of them, one of each primary color, but only the red one has ever been found."

"It's locked," Clayton said, trying the door.

Beep, beep, beep. "There's a message on my MRVD," Clayton said, as he pressed the button to retrieve it. "It's from Thila Mae! It says:

A short cut is always

In front of your eyes

The right way, the wrong way

It's no surprise

S-S-S-W-W-W-O-O-O-S-S-S-H-H-H!! The big, red door swung open.

"Whoa! Cool, look at that," Clayton shouted, peering through the entryway.

"*Shhhh*," Kalya warned. "Quiet."

Clayton gave Kalya a puzzled look and quietly climbed over the threshold and onto the path that led to the grove of towering pikdle trees.

"Now can we talk?" Clayton whispered.

"Yes, I just didn't want us to wake up the door."

"Is it alive?"

"Not exactly. Let's just say it is aware," Kalya answered, cryptically.

"It's getting dark in these trees. I'm going to turn on my Nocto-Vision," Clayton said, pressing the orange button on his MRVD. "How are you going to see?"

"With my eyes. Fivskews have excellent night vision," Kalya replied proudly, heading into the dense growth of towering pikdle trees.

"So why did you perfect the Nocto-Vision if you don't need it?" Clayton asked, running to catch up.

"Yes, well, er…I thought I could add an invention of my own to it," Kalya said, stumbling over his words. "But I'm not sure it works. I hear water, don't you?" he asked, changing the subject.

"It must be up ahead," Clayton said. "Let's hurry!"

Chapter 33

Chaos?

"Whoa! What's that?" Clayton asked, as they emerged from the stand of pikdle trees.

"What's what?"

"That thing up there. Look!" Clayton pointed to the sky.

"It is Thila Mae!" Kalya replied. Thila Mae floated down gracefully and disappeared behind the rise of the hill.

They hurried after her, and soon caught sight of Annie and Ralph on the banks of The Wide River. "Annie! Ralph!" Clayton shouted, running towards them. Annie and Ralph were bent over the sides of a tiny canoe.

"You made it! Just in time," Annie beamed up at them.

"We're almost finished." She picked up three miniature paddles and returned them to their place under one of the seats. Then she and Ralph lifted up the little canoe, flipped it over, and placed it upside down on its berth. Ralph looked surprisingly steady standing upright on his two hind legs.

"What are you doing?" asked Clayton.

"I'll explain in a sec. Follow me," Annie answered, gesturing to the stand of pikdle trees behind Clayton and Kalya.

"But we just came from there," Clayton protested. "I want to check out the river."

"Not now," Annie insisted, grabbing Clayton's arm.

"*Psst!* Over here!" Thila Mae beckoned from her perch high up in the pikdle trees, trying, but failing, to keep her voice at a whisper. The pikdle trees stood too close together for Thila Mae to spread her wings and glide to the clearing below, so she began awkwardly hopping her way down from branch to branch. Each time she landed, the branch beneath her groaned and creaked under the weight of her enormous frame.

"This way,"' Annie ordered, still holding Clayton firmly by his arm and leading him into the trees to join Thila Mae.

"Greetings," smiled Thila Mae, balancing on one spindly leg. Then turning to Clayton she planted both feet firmly on the ground and reached out a long feathery wing. "Pleasure to meet you Clayton. Hold onto this," she said, handing him a small, purple plastic egg.

"What's this? Er…nice to meet you too," Clayton replied,

remembering his manners, but too enthralled by the egg to look up at Thila Mae.

"It's an egg," Thila Mae answered. "Purple like those dedian seeds. Good work getting them back, by the way. Purple is a fun color don't you think? Although I don't like to pick favorites. With colors that is. You take food, I don't feel bad. But colors, that's a different story. Don't want one to feel left out. Left out. Like left might feel if you always pick right. Speaking of food, I'm getting hungry. You wouldn't happen to have…"

"Thila!" Kalya interrupted.

"Right you are," said Thila Mae. "Better wait. Figure The Three will be back in twenty minutes." She folded her tall, awkward body into a seated position on the ground, her long legs tucked under her, her feet sticking out behind.

Clayton stared wide-eyed at Annie. *Thila Mae is one weird bird*, his expression seemed to say.

Annie smiled back knowingly, sat on the ground next to Thila Mae, blew her bangs out of her eyes, and began to explain the Legend of the Elements, the discovery of The Three, and how she and Ralph planned to stop them. "We're going to put out the handheld fireball, and then they won't have all five elements. That's why we painted…"

"*Shhhhhh*…." Ralph warned in a whisper. "Look! Over there!" They peered through the branches and watched the tiny canoe rise up, flip over, and float through the air towards the water's edge. "It must be The Three!"

"Wait!" Clayton said, urgently. "We don't have to put out the handheld fireball! They don't have Chaos anymore because I brought back the dedian plants and seeds. The

Chaos that was created no longer exists."

"What?" Annie asked.

"I found out Dennis was growing dedian seeds on Earth. Once I brought them back here, The Scrolls stopped disintegrating—including the fragment The Three stole!"

"So, they only have four elements," Annie deduced, watching the canoe float out into the river. "I wish we could see what they're doing!"

"Go on," Thila Mae said, poking Kalya with the tip of her wing. "Let them try it."

"Try what?" Annie asked.

"Press your Nocto-Vision button five times," Kalya said, hesitantly.

"One, two, three, four, five," Annie and Clayton counted out quietly, as they each pressed their orange buttons.

"Wow!" Clayton whispered, blinking his eyes in amazement. "I see them. They're like blurry shadows."

"My invention, it works," Kalya said, astonished.

"They're in the canoe," Annie whispered.

"Wait, something's happening….the canoe….it's rocking. Now it's turning back towards the shore."

"They must have discovered that the piece of scroll they have is restored," Kalya said. "They're rowing back."

"They can't make it. The current's too strong," said Clayton. "It's sweeping them back towards the falls."

"And they're stuck to the sap we painted inside the

canoe! Just like flies on flypaper," said Annie, no longer bothering to whisper.

"I can't see the canoe anymore," Clayton shouted. "They must have gone over the falls!"

They all raced to the shore for one last look while Thila Mae soared high into the sky tracing one figure eight after another.

Chapter 34
Tracking Zoom

"That takes care of that," hollered Thila Mae from the sky. "Time to celebrate. Wish I had my trumpet with me. Drat. Hear that alarm ringing. Bet those darn palm fruit are hitting the circuit frames again. Makes the Travel current malfunction every time. Need to go. Duty calls. Where did I put my…" she said, starting into one more figure eight.

"Goodbye," Clayton shouted, waving up at her.

"Thanks for everything," Annie added.

"Favor less words. Nor let more time get old," Thila Mae shouted down, her voice fading as she finished her last loop and flew off.

"What is she talking about?" asked Clayton.

"They must be anagrams," Annie answered. "Thila Mae loves them."

"I've got to go tell Mortimer we stopped them!" said Kalya. "After you," he gestured toward the stand of pikdle trees.

"That's it!" said Annie, proudly. "'Nor let more time get old' is 'need to go tell Mortimer!'"

"How did you do that so fast?" Clayton asked. "I only know, 'evil' is 'live' and 'mood' is 'doom,'" he added.

Annie smiled, shrugged her shoulders, and started down the dark path.

"I can't see anything. My Nocto-Vision doesn't work, does yours?" Clayton asked, fumbling with his MRVD.

"The Tracking Zoom you used to see The Three must still be on," said Kalya. "Hold down the orange button for two seconds—it will revert back to normal Nocto-Vision."

"How did the Tracking Zoom work anyway?" asked Annie. "I mean, how did the MRVD know what we wanted to see?"

"With this tracker sticker," Kalya answered, holding up a small gray square. "I gave Ralph one to stick to the outside of the canoe. Once in place, the Nocto-Vision narrows the field of vision to a radius of 20 feet around the sticker. The effect lasts one hour."

"It looked like a spot light. But how did it work? Aren't Disruptors invisible?" Clayton asked.

"Disruptors emit heat, so when your Nocto-Vision was focused on a small area, your eye saw the movements The Three made."

"Hey, I figured the other one out," Annie exclaimed. "It's 'savers of worlds!'"

"Huh?"

"'Favor less words' translates into 'savers of worlds'!"

"Thila Mae, is so clever," Kalya chuckled.

Ralph charged ahead down the path. They hiked on in silence, Kalya still amazed that his untried invention had actually worked, Annie trying to come up with an anagram sentence of her own, and Clayton eager to let Mr. Ness know the rescued dedian plants and seeds had reversed the damage to the Scroll fragment.

"There's the red door," Clayton shouted, running up the path. Instinctively, he tried the door knob. The door was unlocked.

They stepped over the threshold, closed the door tightly behind them, and hiked on. When they reached the marsh, they slogged through the mud and muck to the rowboat.

Annie rowed to The Jenny N. Clayton secured the rowboat in the hold, and they all jumped into the water to clean off. Once the four had climbed into the cabin and Kalya had set The Jenny N's course for Nessen, Clayton described the game of "three team otter ball" he had watched from the air Travel Current on his way to the Reflective Reef.

....

It was dusk when The Jenny N finally reached Nessen. The colorful sky reminded Clayton of the dazzling display of lights he had seen when he hovered above the rowboat and the horseshoe-shaped trail they had left behind. It was then he remembered what the Reflective Reef had hinted—that the sky held the answers to the questions he had asked, and perhaps to ones he did not yet know.

The End

Glossary

A **Anagram** Rearrangement of a word, phrase, or sentence to form another word, phrase, or sentence: "the eyes," an anagram for "they see."

B **B. B. Gene** Old wooly-haired creature who lives in the Forest of Gruwin. Sometimes goes by the name of B.B.

Bit Joiner Shiny metal disc stamped with the letters N, Z, and U. Required for the proper functioning of an air Travel Current.

Breg Bulbs Vegetable-like plants. Grow beneath the soil in the southern part of Tondore Island. Ripen every mid-afternoon when they rise to the surface. Only thing the Disruptors are known to eat.

Brown Snake Meeting Hall Large cave in Brown Snake Inlet where the brown snakes assemble to discuss important community matters.

D **Dennis** Classmate of Annie and Clayton. Nephew of Franco Dismali (deceased).

Disruptors Mischievous invisible creatures of Tilania and the Underworld. They leave a star-shaped mark after playing practical jokes or harmless pranks to indicate their involvement. *See The Three.*

Doors of Tondore Shortcuts on Tondore Island. Three exist, each painted a primary color. Only the red one has ever been located. Their origin and creator are unknown.

E

Earth World where Annie and Clayton reside.

Elephant Tulips Name Mr. Ness gave the flowers whose tulip-like blooms resemble tiny elephant heads. Native to Nessen. Began growing on the banks of Five-Sided Lake following a Disruptor-caused flood.

F

Five-Sided Lake Lake in Tondore Island on the western edge of the Forest of Gruwin. The Wide River empties into it via The Great Falls.

Fivskew Sea creature living in the Underworld. Resembles a cross between a turtle and a hermit crab.

Forest of Gruwin Vast forest on Tondore Island.

Franco Dismali Mr. Ness's old lab partner who was killed by a falling tree after an earthquake on the Isle of Hearts.

G

Grey Island Only island in the Underworld where no water Travel Current flows.

Gust Blocker Kalya's invention that makes it possible to transport objects on the air Travel Currents. Shooting the Gust Blocker in front of an object releases it from the Travel Current. *See TC Catapult.*

I

Indicator Rocks Three-tiered rock formations which indicate the entry points into air Travel Currents of the Underworld.

Inner Chamber Where The Scrolls are kept in the Portal of Time. Only the Scribes are allowed entry. *See Scribes, Portal of Time, The Scrolls.*

Isle of Hearts Anomalous heart-shaped island of the Underworld that is located in Tilania. The physical laws of the Underworld govern the Isle of Hearts. *See Settlement of the Isle of Hearts.*

Itty-Bitty Robots Small robots Mr. Ness invented; built and programmed to perform simple tasks. Approximately the size of a soda can. Annie named the three on Earth Bo, Sunny, and Clint.

Kalya Renown Fivskew scientist and inventor. He led the research team who upgraded Keriam to save the Underworld. *See TC Catapult, Gust Blocker, and Tracking Zoom.*

Keepers Another name for the three Scribes of Brown Snake Inlet: Lady Abigail, Timothy the Elder, and Simon. They are the recorders, keepers, and protectors of The Scrolls. Only Keepers can travel through the waters of the Portal of Time to enter the Inner Chamber.

Keriam Weather machine of the Underworld. Purpose is to lessen the force and severity of powerful storms and natural disasters. Recently updated by Kalya and his team of scientists, it reduced the power of the deadliest tidal wave on record.

Legend of the Elements Ancient legend of Tilania and the Underworld. Warns that if Chaos and the other four elements: Earth, Water, Fire and Air are taken over The Great Falls, Tilania and the Underworld would be thrown into total confusion and disarray.

Leliac Falls Popular outdoor recreation spot one hour from Oakville.

M

Mortimer Brown snake who is Principal Spokesnake of Brown Snake Inlet. Married to Tallulah. Sent Annie and Clayton message, "Trouble! Scrolls. Keepers can't! Suspicion, Disruptors! Assist POST-HASTE!!"

Mr. Ness Scientist and Inventor. Prefers to be called by his first name, Herman.

Mrs. Ness Mr. Ness's wife, also known as Aunt Jenny. Communicated with Mr. Ness via tea leaves during his ten year disappearance.

MRVD: Multi Recording Visual Device Handheld computer whose functionality resembles a smart phone. Invented by Mr. Ness before cell phones were developed.

N

Nessen Small Island in Western Tilania where Mr. Ness built his research hut.

Nocto-Vision Added feature on the MRVD that allows its user to see in the dark. Originally conceived by Mr. Ness; completed by Kalya.

Norps Vegetable-like plant. Grows near the settlement on the Isle of Hearts. *See wetzel.*

No-see-ums Tiny biting flies on Earth. Also known as midges, sand flies, and punkies. Often found near large bodies of water and in wooded mountainous areas. Barely visible to the naked eye, but can often be seen traveling in swarms.

P

Passageway Narrow slide-like passage between Tilania and the Underworld.

Pikdle Tree Grove A horseshoe-shaped grove of pikdle trees in the Forest of Gruwin near the banks of The Wide River.

Portal of Time Passageway a Scribe must swim through to gain entry into the Inner Chamber where The Scrolls are kept.

R

Ralph Mr. Ness's dog and lab assistant. Able to speak on Tilania but not on Earth. Fur occasionally displays patterns which can be "read" for clues and meanings.

Reflective Reef Reef in the Underworld that functions like an oracle or fortune-teller. Functionality includes the prediction of weather patterns and natural disasters. Source of a wide range and breath of knowledge regarding the Underworld, Tilania, and Earth.

Reflective Reef Institute of Learning
Underworldian school dedicated to the study of the Reflective Reef. Curriculum includes Reef image interpretation and study of ecosystems and historical uses. Graduates are charged with lifelong commitment to the preservation and maintenance of the Reef.

Rock Timer Component of Keriam. Must be properly synchronized for the machine to operate correctly.

S

Screen Glasses Special glasses Fivskews wear to increase their typing speed and enhance their ability to discern visual connections.

Scribes The keepers and protectors of The Scrolls since time immemorial. Three in number, currently: Lady Ablgail, Timothy the Elder, and Simon. One Scribe is chosen to enter the Inner Chamber of the Portal of Time on the 11th day of each month at the second 11th hour; they unfurl The Scrolls, and record the future of Tilania and the Underworld until the next date of entry.

....

Settlement of the Isle of Hearts Scientific colony on the Isle of Hearts built for the study of Earth. Inhabited by a group of Underworldians. Abandoned following an earthquake.

....

Solano Bay Bay on the northwest side of Tondore Island, where the path to the Forest of Gruwin begins.

....

T **Tallulah** Brown snake. Mortimer's wife.

....

Tapedum Lucidum Extra layer of tissue in the eyes of some animals that allows them to see in the dark.

....

TC Catapult Kalya's invention that makes it possible to transport objects on the air Travel Currents. Its lever, when pulled, throws an object into the path of the Travel Current. *See Gust Blocker.*

....

The Great Falls Falls on The Wide River that empty into Five-Sided Lake on Tondore Island. *See the Legend of the Elements.*

....

The Jenny N Research boat built by Mr. Ness in Tilania. Served as his laboratory and his home.

....

The Ness Theory of Travel Mr. Ness's form of travel that uses desire and concentration.

....

The Scrolls Parchment rolls kept in the Inner Chamber accessed through the Portal of Time. Scribes record the past and future of Tilania and the Underworld on the 11th hour of the 11th day of every month. *See Inner Chamber, Portal of Time, Scribes.*

The Ten Clans of Brown Snake Inlet Comprise the population of Brown Snake Inlet. Each clan has a representative in Council: Archibald, Clarissa, Ezra, Mildred, Jeremiah, Priscilla, Maximilian, Rebecca, Wallace, and Victoria.

The Three Name given to the three corrupt Disruptors who planned on using their knowledge of the Legends of the Elements to take over Tilania and the Underworld.

The Tidal Wave Deadliest tidal wave to occur in the Underworld.

The Wide River River beginning on the western side of Tondore Island. It traverses the central valley empting into Five-Sided Lake via The Great Falls. *See Five-Sided Lake, The Great Falls.*

Thila Mae Technician Large pink bird. Technician or mechanic of the air Travel Currents in the Underworld. Thila Mae Techician is anagram for "The Tilania Mechanic." Brother Max has the same responsibilities for the water Travel Currents.

Thimbit Tool of Thila Mae's. Resembles an old fashion eggbeater without the handle. Use unknown.

Three Team Otter Ball Name made up by Clayton to describe game played in the water by otter-like creatures. Two teams play on either side of a net held by a third team. Official rules not confirmed.

Tilania World where Mr. Ness spent over ten years in exile following his mysterious disappearance from Earth.

Tondore Island Island explored and mapped by Mr. Ness. *See the Forest of Gruwin, The Wide River, The Great Falls.*

Tracking Zoom Feature of Nocto-Vision. Invented by Kalya. Activation narrows the field of Nocto-Vision to a radius of 20 feet centered around a tracker sticker. Programmed for a maximum of one hour's duration. Allows detection of all heat emitting objects.

Travel Currents Air and water devices constructed for rapid transport between the main destinations in the Underworld. Air currents work like a pulley system. Once an air current reaches its destination, it slows, turns, and begins its return trip. Water currents travel in one direction only.

Tributaries Small streams that flow into a larger body of water. *See The Wide River and Brown Snake Inlet.*

U **Underworld** The World below Tilania that is reached by traveling down the Passageway.

W **Wetzel** Vegetable-like plant. Grows beneath the soil in Tilania and the Underworld. Similar in taste to a banana.

Here's a sneak peek at

The Third Journey,

the third book in the Tilania Traveler Series.

We hope you enjoy it!

....

For more information, visit us at:

www.TheTilaniaTravelers.com

Chapter 1

New Travelers

"Why is Clayton here so early?" Sunny asked, peering out the workshop window, her body tilted forward, her forehead pressed against the glass. She was standing on top of a wobbly pile of odds and ends on the workshop bench so she could see into the Ness's kitchen.

"Shhh…I'm trying to sleep!" Clint complained.

"He shouldn't be here yet," Sunny explained. "It is only 1:30."

"Why do you care? Be quiet! I'm trying to sleep." Clint repositioned himself next to Bo and the light dimmed from his eyes. He had gone off-line.

"Lazy, good for nothing," Sunny muttered to herself, as she carefully climbed down from her perch. The doorknob turned and Sunny froze, dimming her eyes so that she would appear to be off-line too.

Clayton, talking on his cell phone, opened the workshop door.

"Hey. Slow down Annie. Start again, I didn't catch that!" he said, stopping at the threshold.

"It's due when? I thought you said…

"We have to reprogram them by then?

"Okay. Okay. Calm down. I'll find Mr. Ness and ask him. I'll call you back.

"Bye…yes, I will…" Clayton's voice trailed off as he turned, closed the workshop door, and walked back towards the house.

Sunny snapped to attention, her eyes flickering back on. "Get up!" she cried, her voice tinny and flat. "Get up." She stretched out a shiny metal arm and poked Bo and Clint who sat leaning against each other, limp and lifeless on the workbench. "We've got to get out of here!"

Clint and Bo shook themselves awake, slowly straightened into a standing position, and stared wide-eyed at Sunny, waiting for their voices to reactivate.

"That's what you woke us up for?" Clint asked, peering at the small object lying in Sunny's open hand. "The stamp?"

"No! I woke you up because they are going to reprogram us! The stamp is our way out."

"Our way out? Our way of what?" Bo asked, slowly rolling his head around to stretch out his neck.

"Reprogramming! Haven't you been listening? Mr. Ness has been talking about this for weeks. They're going to wipe our memories and upload the stuff that Annie has been coding. If this happens, there is no guarantee that the stuff we learned on our own will be left untouched! We could be zombies for the rest of our lives!"

"Now Sunny," Bo said, in his slow drawl. "Get a hold of yourself. Let's think about this."

"We don't have time to think…" Sunny began.

"Shhhhh!" Clint interrupted. "Someone's coming!"

Clint and Bo slumped back down and leaned against each other once again, while Sunny resumed her erect, alert position beside them.

The door of the workshop swung open, and Clayton rushed in. He barely noticed the robots as he grabbed a pile of papers off the workbench. "Mr. Ness says we can do it tomorrow," he said into his phone, as he spun around and ran out, slamming the door behind him.

"What did he mean 'do it tomorrow?'" Clint asked, lifting himself up and swiveling his head towards Sunny. "Was he talking about us?"

"Yup. Sure was," said Bo, answering for Sunny.

"I keep telling you, if we stay here we are going to get re-programmed!"

"So what? Maybe the new stuff they program will be cool," Clint replied. "I'm sick of always doing the same boring things. If I have to make one more paper airplane or pot of coffee I'm going to barf (if I knew how to, that is). Besides, I like Clayton and Annie. They are fine humans."

"It has nothing to do with liking them or not. I like them too. But, we can't let them know we can think on our own, and there is no guarantee that reprogramming us won't wipe out everything from our memories."

"Everything?" Clint asked.

"Everything!" Sunny repeated.

"But how are we going to jump?" Clint protested. "We haven't been programmed to."

"Shoot, Clint," said Bo. "The lady's right. We got to save our skin. Can't hurt to try!"

"Suppose we can't figure out how to come back?" asked Clint.

Sunny, ignoring Clint, shuffled stiffly across the length of the cluttered workbench to the microscope, and clamped the stamp into position under the magnifying lens. "Are you coming or what?"

"Yes ma'am," said Bo. "Clint, get your boots movin'. We're gonna see what this Tilania place is all about."

"Oh, alright," said Clint, shuffling over to join them.

Sunny looked at Bo and Clint and smiled. "So what you do is, close you eyes, count to ten and…"

Before she could finish, Bo swung his arms back, bent his legs and jumped. Sunny gasped as she watched him rise higher and higher, become smaller and smaller, and disappear.

"Come on, your next," Sunny said, shoving Clint forward.

"Fine," he answered. Then imitating Bo he closed his eyes, counted, and jumped. As he turned back to smile triumphantly at Sunny, he saw the door of the workshop open and Mr. Ness walk in.

·······························

Made in the USA
San Bernardino, CA
11 January 2015